THE MUSLIMAH WHO FELL TO EARTH

the MUSLIMAH
who FELL to EARTH

personal stories by
CANADIAN MUSLIM WOMEN

Edited by Saima S Hussain

MAWENZI
HOUSE

We acknowledge the support of the Canada Council for the Arts for our publishing program. We also acknowledge support from the Government of Ontario through the Ontario Arts Council.

ONTARIO ARTS COUNCIL
CONSEIL DES ARTS DE L'ONTARIO
an Ontario government agency
un organisme du gouvernement de l'Ontario

Canada Council   Conseil des arts
for the Arts   du Canada

Cover art: *Pure-Fatimaa* by Meliha Teparic. Acrylic on canvas, 150x150 cm, 2006. Reproduced with permission of Meliha Teparic.

Cover design by Peggy Stockdale.

Library and Archives Canada Cataloguing in Publication

The Muslimah who fell to earth : personal stories by Canadian Muslim women / edited by Saima S Hussain.

ISBN 978-1-927494-82-0 (paperback)

1. Muslim women--Canada. 2. Muslim women--Canada--Biography. 3. Muslim women--Canada--Social conditions. I. Hussain, Saima S., editor

HQ1170.M88 2016   305.48'6970971   C2016-904420-3

Printed and bound in Canada by Coach House Printing.

Mawenzi House Publishers Ltd.
39 Woburn Avenue (B)
Toronto, Ontario M5M 1K5
Canada
www.mawenzihouse.com

Contents

⁓

Introduction

SAIMA S HUSSAIN

IN THE LATE 1930s Hilwi Hamdon approached the mayor of
Edmonton, John Fry, for a plot of land to build a mosque for
the growing Muslim community of the city. He agreed to give
the land if she could come up with the $5,000 needed for the con-
struction. Hilwi went around the city with her friends asking for
donations, which she received from Muslims, Jews, and Christians.
On December 12, 1938 the Al-Rashid Mosque was inaugurated by
Mayor Fry. It was the first mosque built in Canada.

In 1988 Lila Fahlman, founder of the Canadian Council of
Muslim Women (CCMW) led a campaign to preserve this now historic mosque by transporting it to Fort Edmonton Park. Fahlman
and her group worked hard to raise the $75,000 needed to move the
mosque, and even harder to overcome the opposition to designate
it a heritage building. In 1991 this little mosque on the prairie finally
found a permanent home in the park.

It was Muslim women who built Canada's first mosque, and it
was their successors who later saved it for posterity. They played
a vital role in the establishment of Alberta's Muslim community,
and have in this way left an indelible mark in Canada's collective
history. It is unfortunate that the names and life stories of these pio-
neers are largely unknown.

In 1938 there were an estimated 700 Muslims in Canada, roughly half of them women. In 1991 the number of Muslims had risen to 253, 265, approximately half of whom were women. The census of 2011 counted 513,380 Muslim women, 28.5 % percent of them born in Canada. By 2030 the population of Muslim women is expected to exceed one million with an even greater percentage born in Canada.

The intention of this book is to document the lives of contemporary Canadian Muslim women in their own words. The idea for it came after a friend at work confided that I was the only Muslim woman she knew. "We live in Mississauga so surely you must be joking," I told her. "I wish," she replied solemnly. "I exchange smiles with them on the street or at the mall. I even exchange a 'hi!' with some at my kids' school or the pool, but we never talk, so I don't know them."

Over the next eighteen months I reached out far and wide across the country, talking on the phone to women I had never (and still haven't) met, chatting with them about their experiences, sometimes encouraging and sometimes cajoling them to write their stories. I asked them to share their personal experiences relating to what it meant for them to be Canadians and Muslims, to tell readers details about their lives, their concerns, and their aspirations. A few were not comfortable disclosing personal details, but others immediately came on board. All of them agreed that there was an urgent need for Canadian Muslim women to share their own stories in their own voices and be heard.

I took considerable efforts to reflect the diversity of Canada's Muslim population in this volume, nevertheless the representation is by no means complete. There are many stories that remain to be told, by women from various other sects, ethnic groups, and beliefs within the growing Muslim communities.

This book has been a labour of love for me and for every woman who has contributed her story to it. We dedicate it to the enterprising women who came before us and to the powerful women who will follow us.

Mississauga, Ontario

Standing My Ground

KIRSTIN SABRINA DANE

Crossing the Line

THE SOUND OF my heart threatened to drown out the imam leading the sunset prayer. I suddenly found myself in the centre of the room, and even though my eyes never left the direction of the qiblah, the invisible path to Mecca, I saw everything with a new awareness. Rows of men stood in front of me. Some fidgeted, some swayed to the Quranic recitation, some wore jeans, while others had opted for more formal wear. My oldest daughter darted across the room, running freely through the space that separates the men from the women. Still not old enough to officially join us in prayer, I wondered if she could nevertheless feel the heat of violation and outrage pouring from my body as she flitted around the mosque. Or if she had witnessed my transgression, the moment I left the line of women to step into the men's section and protest against those who had attempted to shut me behind a barrier.

We arrived earlier that evening for a fund-raising dinner. It was a welcoming and bright atmosphere with about 250 people and a mix of smiling and somber faces. Children ran freely between the men's and women's sections, and a few adults milled about while a speaker droned on about the Islamic duty to be charitable and to help the less fortunate.

After I grabbed the diaper bag from my husband, we said goodbye to each other and went to our respective sections in the main prayer hall. He went to the front of the room with the men, while I took my two daughters to pray in the back with the women. A line of curtains divided us.

The barrier was set up with movable panels—giving women the choice to pray hidden from the men, or to pray unhindered by a barrier. I took the girls and joined the front row of women, purposefully positioning myself at an open panel. I pulled out my trusty backpack filled with crafts and activities, and facilitated some quiet play for my girls, and then a few other children joined them as news spread that we had sparkly stickers.

Over the past thirty years, the separation of men and women in North America has increased dramatically, using either some kind of partition between them or relegating the women to a separate room, such as a balcony or a basement. The reasons are complicated, ranging from cultural-religious expectations, to personal preference. Connected to the separation is the unfortunate and gradual exclusion of women from the mosque, and the creation of hostile religious spaces. Women are simply not welcome in the men's section. The separation aims to silence and shut women out of the community under the guise of sacred personal space.

Eventually, the fund-raiser came to a close and the call to prayer rang out over the congregation. People began shuffling and straightening their prayer lines. A few women closed privacy panels. I remained standing at an open one. A woman closed the panel next to me, but another interjected and said she wanted to pray with it open. Open. Closed. Open. Closed. There was a stand-off and eventually the woman who wanted it closed prayed elsewhere.

While we waited for the imam to start, I noticed two men looking over at my open panel. They pointed and motioned for the curtain to come down. I immediately mentioned this to the other two women next to me, making sure they were okay praying with an open panel. They were.

The prayer started. We bowed in reverence to the Almighty. But when I rose, a smirking, indignant teenage boy stood before me. He reached up with his hand and closed the curtain, shrouding us behind a panel of peach and white linen.

Immediately, I broke from the line of women, tossed aside the curtain, and stepped into the men's section.

So there I stood, alone in the space that separates the men from the women, eyes planted firmly on the presence of God in my mind. The youth who shut me behind a barrier gaped widely and then walked away deflated—perhaps ashamed, knowing that he was the cause of my protest.

My daughter zipped by and then joined me on my left side. I glanced down and she looked up at me, beaming. I melted and felt stronger with her near me. Eventually my sister-in-law joined me on my right. In that moment I could have cried. While trying to concentrate on the prayer, a part of me wondered what was going to happen next. Would the imam say something? Would people escort me and my daughters out of the mosque?

After the prayer was over we all sat in silent reflection. No one moved. No one screamed. No one attacked us. I turned to my sister-in-law and asked why she joined me. She shrugged and said, "No one should pray alone."

That's when I realized how separated I had become from the Muslim community; that while I was connected to Islam my connection to the mosque was severed.

The Opening

When I was an impressionable, young convert, I wore my Islam on my sleeve. I'd openly play with my silver "Allah" necklace and pepper my conversations with recognizable "Muslim-Arabic" catchphrases in the hopes that someone would question me about my faith, just so I could tell them about the awesomeness of Islam.

I worked with the Muslim Student Association, spoke passion-
ately about my conversion at lectures, and helped promote Islam
by handing out easily digestible pamphlets on "Women in Islam,"
"Science in Islam," and "Misconceptions in Islam." In turn, my
new community inundated me with advice on the "proper" way
to be Muslim, and high on faith, I didn't delve deeply into why I
suddenly had to pray five times a day, fast, speak Arabic, and wear
hijab. I had accepted a new universal Truth and took everything at
face value.

At some point during my early acceptance of Islam, I lost who
I was as an individual in my attempt to become the "perfect Muslimah." The community gave me a standard, broad script to read
from and I implanted a record in my mind that, to this day, plays a
list of proper conduct, *haraam* and *halal* living, and the "right" way
to worship as a Muslim. Any deviation from this list meant that I
was not a real Muslim. But there was a constant disconnect between
what I believed I should practice and how the world worked around
me; between what I expected of my Muslim community and what
was actually put in place. My devotion became burdensome and
disappointing. My biggest struggle was with hijab.

I can still remember the chills that raced across my skin when I
made the intention to put it on. The moment I spoke the words to
God, I felt a comforting weight descend all around me—like someone had wrapped me in a cloak. At first, I made a promise saying
that I would never take it off. But I quickly backtracked, augment-
ing my intention with a promise to "try to keep it on" and asking
for divine help to do so.

Back in the early 2000s, there were no websites showcasing the
diversity of hijab, or YouTube videos with fashion-trending hijabi-
stas strutting their stuff on New York and Indonesian catwalks,
or even viral images of badass Star Wars hijabi cosplay. The vast
majority of sources at the time equated a woman's piety with hijab
and her duty to God to "protect her inner pearl." They emphasized the stripping away of makeup, jewelry, colour, perfume, and

adornments, parts of my former life that helped me to express my creativity and personality. So I bought myself drab blacks, browns, and navy blues, and a whole new "modest" wardrobe. I was recreating myself, embracing what I believed was a truly "Islamic" way of life. I was enthusiastically supported by friends who wanted to see me succeed and become a better Muslim.

I lowered my gaze. I stopped talking to men. I was trying to become invisible, but instead attracted the attention of non-Muslims who were confused to see a white woman with *that thing* on my head, or those who used me as an opportunity to vent anti-Muslim bigotry. I also caught the attention of the occasional Muslim mosque Auntie on the prowl for a good, pious wife for her son. And while my new identity was supported by community accolades, my sense of self shattered.

It was exhausting trying to maintain the image of the "pious Muslimah"—especially when all around me I saw other Muslim women living authentically, seemingly at peace with their religion and their identities. As a convert, it seemed that wearing makeup or short-sleeve t-shirts, celebrating Christmas, or listening to Western music were no longer options for me. I looked at my sisters-in-Islam with longing and loss, because they could apparently do these things and not have their faith questioned. They would always be Muslim. If I did anything outside of the "ideal," I was corrected, and I feared being labelled as a fraud or an imposter, when my faith was just as real.

It would be years before I became close friends with another female convert and learn that I wasn't the only one feeling pressure to eschew Western culture and activities or beliefs that made up my personality. And eventually I met other Muslim women who helped cure my "convertitis" and taught me that it was totally acceptable to listen to Radiohead while cruising in a car on the way to the mosque. And that you could reconcile faith with feminism.

Being a Muslim woman means more than existing as a single ideal. Some Muslim women are incredibly pious and don't wear the hijab. Some are single mothers or have chosen to be happily unmarried. Muslim women can be queer, transgender, and cisgender. They might support blended families by working three jobs, home-schooling, or coaching the local soccer team. They wear niqab and champion women's rights. Muslim women are immigrants, converts, second-generation Canadians. They're authors, activists, artists, doctors, politicians, and feminists. They get their nails done, bake cookies, own too many cats, and go to the gym. Women choose to wear the hijab for amazingly diverse reasons, cultural, political, as protest, solace, protection or fashion expression. Whether I wear an abaya, a fashionable turban twist, a face veil, or take everything off completely, no one knows just how much I love God.

Of course, people also use the hijab to oppress and control women, and it is absolutely a target for Islamophobia and an excuse for prejudice. But it is not a piece of cloth that oppresses women. Oppression comes from discrimination, exploitation, inequality, domestic violence, and religiously justified misogyny.

Half of Faith

Possibly the easiest thing I found in the practice of my faith was getting married. Alhamdulillah, I was blessed with the right partner and, together, we have created three amazing children.

Before meeting my husband I had no cultural ties or extensive community to introduce me to potential suitors, and wasn't quite sure where I was supposed to find a partner. I knew that I was a triple catch: young, white, convert. In the first year of taking on hijab, I had three serious marriage proposals by strangers. I eventually met my husband at university through the Muslim Student Association. And he is my proof that "marriage is half of faith." He makes me a better person and has helped me navigate Islam as well as find my life passions.

He brought music back into my life by encouraging me to relearn the saxophone and by taking me to my very first Alice Cooper concert. He was understanding when I made the (shocking!) choice to wear jeans again or shake up my traditional head scarf and publish a hijab video tutorial. He indulges my geeky hobbies and lets me dress him up like a zombie. He's helping me raise empowered, empathetic, and intelligent children. He loves my phenomenal non-Muslim parents and acknowledges our traditions by celebrating Christmas 'Eid. And when I can't get to the mosque during Ramadan because of the young ones, he stays home with me to watch live streaming prayers from Mecca, or Seeker's Hub lectures.

I think about how we have developed a marriage based on trust, security and equity, and wonder about an Islamic verse saying that "men are the maintainers of women." This is used to justify all sorts of misogynist behaviour, from preventing women from leading prayers, to justifying domestic violence against women. Sometimes it's used to argue that women are restricted to the private sphere of home life, while men are free agents of the public sphere; that the role of men in Islam includes being the king of the household—where his word is law.

"Heaven is at the feet of the mother" and "obeying your mother is a form of worship" are beautiful messages that are frequently drilled into every child, selling a positive role of women-as-mothers in Islam. The Quran tells all believers to honour their parents, specifically mentioning mothers with regards to the struggles of pregnancy and early child care. It makes a point to spell out that both parents should be treated well because birth and weaning are difficult for women.

Willingly or not, women often sacrifice aspects of their spirituality in order to support the family. Many mothers and their children are banished from the main prayer spaces to pray in the "children's rooms." During Ramadan, pregnant or nursing women who choose not to fast may be isolated from the rituals while relied upon to prepare elaborate meals for those who fast, also while caring for multiple children. As if not fasting somehow disqualifies women from participating in any other rituals and community events.

The role of men and women in Islam is not so easily cut-and-dried. The Prophet darned his own socks, allowed children to jump on his back during prayer, held babies, and cleaned his own home. His wives owned businesses, fought on battlefields, and became political leaders, proof for me that family responsibilities shouldn't be easily divided, deflected, devalued, or put only on one person to maintain.

Living Islam

An average day for me is pretty busy. After a morning shower I get dressed and hopefully have enough time to pray before dashing out the door to catch my train. I eat a packed sandwich for lunch and call my mom, thanking her for dealing with my toddler's chronic cough with a German remedy. In the afternoon, I take a break to pray in my workplace "quiet room:" a diversity and religious inclusiveness initiative. On the way back to my desk, I excitedly chat up a colleague about the new Muslim Ms Marvel comic. After work, when my husband comes home with the kids, we play an Arabic-language game while eating a halal chicken dinner. Then when the bedtime chaos subsides, my husband researches a local Islamic Montessori school while I work on making the family Steampunk costumes for the next comic convention.

It's the privileged life of a middle-class, heterosexual, able-bodied, multilingual extended Canadian family. It also seems fairly innocuous that we live in accordance to certain Islamic rules and guidelines, or in other words, the Sharia. But for some, this snapshot illustrates my family's hidden agenda. The "quiet room" at my place of employment is solid proof that multiculturalism in Canada has failed by "tolerating the intolerant Muslim." Considering sending the kids to an Islamic school is proof of extremist indoctrination. And any community work I'm involved with is just a ruse to slowly turn Canada into an Islamic state, especially if it involves dressing up like superheroes.

There's an irrational fear that foreign-based, extremist inter-pretations of Islam are creeping into North America. In response, Muslim parents are being placed into complex situations where they have to communicate positive Muslim identity while deflecting and protecting their children from internalizing negative stereotypes so often used by media and politicians to portray Muslims. Parenting Muslim children now includes providing them with a script on what to do if they're bullied and called a terrorist at school, and not to speak about guns, shootings, or bombings—even if they're only talking about a video game with their friends.

We are lucky to be surrounded by positive images of Mus-lims, to have allies that see beyond the stereotypes, and to live in a city where religious diversity is promoted under the banner of inclusion.

Thankfully, my children are still too young to really understand everything that's going on in the world and I haven't had to shelter them from anything serious. Although, one time when my three-year-old daughter insisted on making "boom" and "crash" noises with her toy cars while we were on a flight to British Columbia, I panicked and probably annoyed even more passengers by suddenly breaking out into a loud and over-exuberant version of "Itsy Bitsy Spider."

Beyond the Barrier

It's heartbreaking to feel like my family doesn't entirely belong to a particular mosque or community—that we don't often join my husband for Friday prayers because I want to limit my children's exposure to hostile prayer spaces, horrible sermons, and barriers.

Mosques are supposed to be the spiritual centre of the community, open to all without criticism, judgement, or dis-crimination, supporting those who need it, fostering equality, and engaging in public service. Instead, many in Canada are physically and spiritually cold, are unfriendly towards the LGBTQ community, are plagued by sectarianism, and struggle to connect with the youth. Some imams produce sermons more concerned with discussing parking and unruly children than domestic violence and sexual assault. And while it is true that you can pray anywhere on the clean Earth, and find spiritual fulfillment in spaces created outside the mosque, one just needs to look at a picture of the swirling masses around the Ka'bah in Mecca to be reminded that prayer is central to Islam, and how important the mosque is as a place of community.

The very first time I attended Friday prayers as a new Muslim, I took a two-hour bus ride and walked in the rain without an umbrella to get there. Women entered the building from a side entrance and we prayed in a small enclosure—practically a box in the main prayer hall. The imam was less than fifty feet away, but I watched him on a closed-circuit television, and strained to hear him. Almost ten years later, in a bright and airy room without barriers, I led a mixed prayer at a gender-inclusive centre in Toronto.

I came to Islam because I found peace in the Quran. Throughout the Quran, God calls, "Oh you who believe . . . " Each verse is a commandment toward living a greater Good: Fear God. Establish the prayer. Stand for Justice. Join together in Peace. Fast. Be patient.

This is the only message I ever needed to hear.

Vast Unknowables

FERRUKH FARUQUI

THERE IS SOMETHING melancholic in the hushed air of a December evening. The long drawn-out winter nights settle with an almost discernable sigh on the heels of raw November days. This recurrent slipping of the year into its final month is soothing in its familiarity. It elicits the contemplation of sorrows, progress, and joys. Although I was born on the arid shores of a crowded coastal city where humanity grows with unchecked fecundity, I think of the north when I think of home.

Landscape, climate, and geography are the vast unknowables that seep into the interstices of my heart and mind. They grip my sensibilities with a light but tenacious hold and give form to the way in which I settle into an inchoate world.

Elemental things like water, air and earth move me to a helpless feeling of rapture. Everything about this country that made me is large. The scale is one of surpassing grandeur. Its dimensions are quoted in tens of thousands, north and south, east and west. And straight up into the third dimension of space into which the jagged Rockies thrust their icy peaks into a thin sky. The endless expanse of land between the shores of three brooding oceans seems impenetrable to outsiders who can scarcely conceive that all of this space is just one country. I grew up on the Prairies, in a province larger than most nations, on the edge of a windswept city colonized by English and French settlers. Later came waves of newcomers who hailed from the British Isles, the Ukraine, Iceland and the Philippines.

How does setting, with its corollaries of physical space, geography both physical and emotional, and the teeming elements shape and define our understanding of the world?

We arrived on an icy March morning at a grey stone building in the heart of Winnipeg's core. We lived in an apartment on the top storey. It was a large, rambling slightly derelict suite, with dull blond hardwood floors, lengths of dark wooden wainscoting and an old marble fireplace with a faded hearth. The white claw-foot bathtub in the echoing bathroom crouched like a beast about to leap on the unwary.

Only two blocks away was the iconic Hudson's Bay Company edifice facing Portage Avenue, with the history of Canadian explorers engraved on its walls. We lived within walking distance of corporate Winnipeg but were excluded from its privilege. Somehow a few families from Pakistan and India managed to find each other in the late 1960s and hold on to their faith. Sunni or Shia, no one cared. I remember a long ago Ramadan in January when these friends crowded into the apartment. The days were short and arctic, the fasting easy with little in the way of thirst or hunger.

My emerging faith was a private one, shaped by the climate and the geography of the prairies where winds blew lonesome. The enormous sky curved concave and seemed a direct conduit to a very present God.

Even in the city, we were never too far from the encroaching plains. In downtown Winnipeg, the wide vistas of Memorial Boulevard were impressive to my childish gaze. There were few skyscrapers and the overarching sky was unobscured by tall buildings. We used to walk down the boulevard to the Manitoba Legislature and stroll the grounds, marvelling at the majestic limestone monument with its golden boy perched atop the dome, and picnic at the base of Queen Victoria's statue, careless of her majesty's stern and regal visage. There were flowering beds of perennials amidst verdant green lawns under the blue sunlit sky of a prairie summer, laced with trailing wispy clouds.

In winter, the lawns became wide expanses of powdery snow, a field of diamonds reflecting the brilliant sunlight.

I remember beauty. The earth around me was a profusion of loveliness, like a woman so richly endowed that she becomes careless of her splendour and lacks all vanity. The breathless air of a winter morning was tremulous and watchful. Like a young girl on the cusp of womanhood, this beauty never paled. It remained as fresh as spring recurring over millennia.

Of course it was disturbing to see the occasional man lying prone behind a bench, or staggering blankly past and to hear the whispered asides about drunken Indians. But to me these indigenous men, sunk into apathy, were not quite hopeless. They had a proud and storied link to the land. This bond, described in textbooks and films, was deeper and more primal than that of the white settlers who later usurped their aboriginal homelands.

Look at an atlas of North America. My first glimpse left me staring in wonder at the pages trying to contain a mammoth continent that spilled over and could not be contained. The topographical maps detail the stunning diversity of the country's ecological regions. Winnipeg is at the centre of this continental land mass, which is held at bay by three restless seas. It's a humble city where no one goes unless they live there. But it embraced me and enfolded me and made me its own.

The climate is a forbidding one, with superficial changeableness and extremes of temperature that swallows up the hapless sojourner into its vast belly. Although I speak of winter with the possessiveness of a jealous lover, all of the seasons charm and delight. Under the balmy skies of June the land blooms into fertile acres glowing with luminous colour. From pink granite outcroppings abutting the indigo waters of glacial lakes, to green needled pines sprouting from bare rock, the temperate loveliness of this province is painted large across the Canadian Shield's broad expanse.

In the Whiteshell region east of Winnipeg we would repair to picnic during the long lazy days of summer. We drove down roads dark with the shadows of spruce and fir and trembling aspen. The boreal forest covers sixty percent of Canada's land mass. This region is sacred to the aboriginal peoples. Thousands of years ago, the ancestors of the Anishinaabe nation traversed this harsh landscape, scarcely disturbing the vast forested plateau with its abundant wildlife. Much later came the voyageurs and fur traders to mine the land of its wealth. The woodsy sounds are subtle—the cool rustling of birch leaves as a July breeze cools the languid air of a midsummer day. The rush of hidden waterfalls and swiftly flowing rivers, coolly pristine, fill listening ears with music.

These are enchanted woods. Benign spirits populate this sacred ground, as remote as can be from the crowded rows of intemperate congregations hectored by impatient mullahs. Like my forerunners I learned to worship in the lofty temples of old growth forests. Kneeling beside gurgling streams that sing their adoration in crystalline notes, I thrill to this evidence of the divine around me.

The great natural theatre of this infinite space speaks of eternity and the transcendence of God. Time and space are governed by laws of physics to order the universe and our lives. We were created of dust, scriptures teach us and now scientists confirm this truth. We are literally made of stardust, astronomers tell us. The gas and dust expelled by the explosion of a dying star contains carbon, hydrogen and other elements which disperse in space to eventually make up all the matter in the universe including human beings and other life. Perhaps that's why when we gaze at the starry sky, we long to return to the cosmos that created us. And why we yearn to achieve union with our maker.

The poet Robert Louis Stevenson wrote of "Green days in forests and blue days at sea," and in his terse lines are echoed the sublime joy of a life lived in synchrony with a deity who is both grand and infinitesimally small.

The 1871 census reported a mere thirteen Canadian Muslims, who were of European origin. In 1966, shortly before our immigration, Winnipeg boasted only 257,000 inhabitants in all. This vast but sparsely populated land, with its brief winter days can spell isolation. Only those acquainted with the endless nights of a northern winter can appreciate its well of solitude. And this solitude means we must make a companion of our souls.

Religion and faith are distinct. I had little exposure to the first, at least as far as Islam went. In school we listened to Bible readings and recited the Lord's Prayer daily. Our friends went to church on Sundays, which were strictly days of rest. There was no Christian embarrassment in discussing God or Christ. No one knew of Muslims or Islam, and since we children didn't either, there was remarkably little tension in our daily lives. Our parents and the few families we knew harboured no resentment of this. In fact they seemed untroubled by the absence of Islam from the national conversation.

I do recall my father performing the morning prayer but paid scant attention. It seemed little more than a puzzling idiosyncracy of his. It had no connection to me. Later I heard him recite the rhythmic verses of the Quran. Its eloquence often makes me weep. I read bits of the English translation daily and the beauty of the text always has the power to arrest me. Certain verses have such force that I read them over and over again, revelling in the words. At these times and in the lingering twilight after sunset and before sunrise, God feels very close.

These are personal experiences, rarely felt in the collective moments in congregation or in the presence of strangers. For me there's a stark divide between the personal and public experiences of faith. I prize the former and fear the latter. Early on, our diminutive community in Winnipeg was a source of strength. We focused on the essentials. Trivialities like women's place and women's bodies and uncovered hair didn't trouble anyone. Neither of my parents sought to impose belief much less ritual upon us. As we grew up we saw our parents fast and perform the daily prayers, recite Quran, and attend Friday services. In the accessible main hall of the mosque we were free to wander at will. We were soporific in our innocence.

But this halcyon time didn't last. Increasing immigration and the growing clout of Saudi clerics and petrodollars combined to precipitate a revolution of sorts in our mosque. Instead of an Arab Spring, it became an Arab Winter. And the frozen wasteland of this perpetual winter has effectively muzzled those whose Islam was questioning, open, and free to interpretation.

Because our father worked from the earliest days as a trustee of the Manitoba Islamic Association we were regularly conscripted into volunteering on all fronts. The year I turned fourteen was when our humble mosque opened its doors. We were ecstatic, after years of hard work raising money, breaking sod and finally building something tangible. We were a mix of ethnicities speaking a variety of languages but remained united. The mosque itself, on a small plot of land in suburban St Vital on Hazelwood Avenue, was modest but wide open and bright with large windows. There was no segregation of women from men. No one seemed threatened by us.

I had never heard of hijab, had never been taught that women must be hidden away, relegated to back rooms or to seedy corridors. But one ominous day we came to the mosque and found a barrier separating the men in front from the women in the back. The older women muttered loud imprecations in their various languages as they slammed open the slats so they could see. The partition was of pale green plastic and left sizable gaps on either end, so that shameless girls like me who sat against the far walls could ignore it and actually see and be seen. The more conservative women would stalk forward and slam the slats shut. And back and forth it would go, feeding on the simmering resentment of ideological divide.

That partition was a declaration of war. The furious tide swept across North America at an accelerated pace as the eighties brought fresh waves of immigrants who concentrated on ritual and dogma. Thus began the war on women. At home no one spoke about gender roles. Yet the contradictions were plentiful and vivid. Our father was the undisputed head of the household who often encouraged and sometimes demanded. He was a fierce proponent of education, especially for women, but his worship of knowledge didn't save him from the baggage of his cultural background.

Mom ran the house and worked full time in a succession of jobs. I looked down upon her with a sort of benign contempt. She wistfully recalled her science courses at her Pakistani convent school, but compared to our dominant father she was a marginal figure. She was a talented chef—she made sublime shami kebabs—but this gift was domestic and therefore patently inferior. When she boarded the plane from Karachi to join her husband overseas, she was a silent wraith-like figure in a black burqa—bare-headed—on whom devolved the responsibility of ferrying three young children across the Atlantic.

It was a solemn homecoming for our timorous mother, who spoke little in those days and whose most characteristic trait was her deference to our father. The large living room in that old apartment building had a bay window looking out onto Balmoral Street, and on bright January days the warm sun streamed in. My mother would spread a roughly woven checkered blanket on the floorboards and lay down in the square of sunlight, willing the warmth to seep into her frozen bones and tide her over till June. She was strikingly lovely but shy and unsure. She had matriculated from the Convent Girls' High School in Renala Khurd, a town in Punjab a hundred kilometres from Lahore. She fondly recalls her time there playing basketball and studying physics. The nuns were mostly kind, she relates, and the girls were mostly Muslim.

But when she came to Canada, her credentials weren't enough to enter the white collar world, so for years she laboured as a seamstress. In her forties she decided to go to college but my father gave her no encouragement. His one ambition was to see all his children, including both daughters, attain academic and professional success, but he showed little interest in the developing mind of his wife.

From fathers and brothers we first learn about men. From mothers and sisters we learn to be women. My father taught me that knowledge was a treasure. I also saw his personal piety and am the ongoing object of his earnest prayers for success, health, and happiness. But I also saw that he judged most women, even the distinguished, as inherently unsuited to assume leadership roles, especially at home. From my mother I learned that the drive to learn cannot be suppressed. She went on to succeed and worked at Manitoba's Legislative Library, meeting and conversing with members of the legislature. I learned, too, that her qualities of tenderness and generosity were no mean gifts to be despised but a rich dower bestowed by God. As I grew into womanhood, and then motherhood, my youthful arrogance abated and my admiration for her grew.

Women's role in Islam is a reliable flashpoint for both Muslims and for western society. The former shrilly pay lip service to our rights while the latter gleefully pronounce us oppressed. Arthur Miller's prescient play *The Crucible* is set in seventeenth century Massachusetts. Hapless victims who were mostly women were suspected of witchcraft and put to death on the flimsy evidence of hysterical Puritan accusers. There are any number of newly minted Puritans holding court in our mosques today. With similar zeal they have routed the old order and with casual arrogance declare themselves to be the true believers.

Where do Muslim women set down their brains when they pass through the women-only entrances to their mosques? Why do they raise funds, volunteer their time, defer to male voices, and accept third-rate spaces? Why do they buy into the lie that within the confines of the mosque, the only intelligence is masculine, and their sole role is to acquiesce?

Still, my human need for fellowship drives me occasionally to the masjid. I enter a space where even the youngest of boys feels he can direct me to the women's door. It's humiliating and degrading. Then with tension steadily mounting it's off to find a spot to sit. I look around at the room which is bare and utilitarian and at women who are smugly covered. The fine carpets and the rich furnishings are reserved for the men's space. Some women look meaningly, even menacingly at my fingernails which are usually painted. I get flustered and forget why I'm here. Instead of concentrating on my devotions, I'm worried about what comes next.

It can be a palpable closing of the ranks against me. The more officious may invade my personal space to touch me or adjust my clothing. In any case the experience serves to isolate and ostracize. It's tough to be a pariah, no matter the century. So instead of remonstrating, I slink away in defeat.

In the silent watches of the night, especially when fasting I feel cherished by God and my spirit expands. But in a house of worship I contract and become small. The limitless horizon outside shrinks to the reality of a cramped back room where instead of thirsting minds I find narrowed thinking and glum faces imprisoned by resentment.

Over my lifetime the spiritual landscape of North American Islam has swung many times a hundred and eighty degrees. From isolated but cohesive outposts shining a welcome light in the fog to an era of exponential Muslim growth we should be glad. But instead I feel besieged. With the idealism of faith I long for that spiritual community called ummah. But with the painful clarity wrought by an adult pragmatism and the bitter reality of contemporary Canadian Islam I see only division. We are straitjacketed by sectarianism and an absence of joy. We cannot escape the effect of civilizational upheavals across the globe, for borders are porous. The mayhem in Muslim majority nations screams on the evening news.

And so the irony grows. The more we try to escape the incursions of the world upon us, the more inexorably it closes round us. And if when cornered we seek solace in our spiritual spaces we find a separate tyranny. Instead of welcome and wisdom we're rebuffed by stern sermons and rigidity of thought. We enter hoping to unfetter our spirits only to hear the echoing clang of shadowy chains. What else can we do but flee?

It has also become clear that our democratic institutions of Parliament, free speech, and the like are not as robust as we had believed. My pride in Canada is based on these pillars. But mainstream society hasn't caught up to the pulsing, dynamic reality of Canadian Muslims. And only a few handpicked partisan spokespersons inform the media's Muslim perspective. This unrepresentative version of Canadian Islam serves to oversimplify a discourse which should be substantive and complex.

The blue hills of Gatineau Park beckon along the parkway that follows the broad waters of the mighty Ottawa River. Across this watery channel which divides Ontario from Quebec, the park is a favourite destination of mine. Here within the national capital region is a green sanctuary of hardy forest and placid lakes. On a forest path we carefully pick our way to avoid tripping on the exposed roots and slippery, moss-covered rock, and clamber down the stony path to sit beside a perfect lake that glimmers glassy green in the sun. This place of crystal air, like the oases dreamed of by medieval desert Arabs is a place untainted by the sophistries of pundits either in the minbar or the newsroom. Its reverent silence is punctuated by the call of the warbler and the song of the thrush or the plop of a frog hopping into the shallow pools at the water's edge.

Both sacred and secular spaces have become jarring places of discord. Here I can retreat to find some peace to nourish my thirsting soul. Here there be gladness yet to beguile my days.

Queering Islam Through Ijtihad

MARYAM KHAN

BEFORE I SHARE my narrative with all of you, I would like to state that my experiences, beliefs, values and opinions do not reflect *all* racialized Muslims who are gender and sexually diverse. Also, my narrative is situated in a specific sociopolitical and her-storical[1] context, and does not speak for *all* racialized Muslim women residing in the west[2]. You as the reader will interpret my narrative through the lenses of your beliefs, values, and experiences which may be based on your subject position. In other words, my narrative will change on who is doing the reading so it is impera-tive to remain cognizant of what becomes attached to my narrative (since it may not belong to me). Through the mere act of writing, I construct myself and others. I want you to read my narrative as resistance (ijtihad), something which may have gloomy aspects to it; but is defined by the resistance and not by marginality. I am thinking of what hooks[3] (2015) has taught me about marginality and resistance. As she states:

> I write these words to bear witness to the primacy of struggle in any situation of domination (even within family life); to the strength and power that emerges from sustained resistance, and the profound convic-tion that these forces can be healing, can protect us

from dehumanization and despair (p. 8).

On Family and Friends

Growing up in a conservative-orthodox Sunni Muslim household, my siblings and I were well versed in how to culturally and religiously perform as Muslims in a large metropolitan city like Toronto. My parents instilled Islamic and cultural values in us, thereby guaranteeing us a respectable social position in the larger Indian, Pakistani, and Bengali Muslim communities. My mother was an active member of the mosque community and we followed suit. At the mosque, there was general discomfort surrounding sex, sexuality, and sexual identity; these subjects were not discussed openly in sermons and at the "water cooler" conversations. Since these topics were also left untouched at home, the most viable option left was receiving information from one's peers and conducting your own research on the internet.

At the masjid, there were innumerable sermons about the perils "out there" like *homosexuality* with quotations from Quran relating to Prophet Lut and Sodom and Gomorrah. As an adolescent it was a perturbing thought for me that God would ordain different rules for each gender. Not *once* in my heart, while hearing homophobic and transphobic sermons, did I conceive that God disapproved of me and would abandon me. I knew God better than those who have gone to *this* Islamic school and studied in *that* country. I experienced God firsthand through my Wali and Rahman's everlasting love, mercies, and compassions. God already told me from the start that I would never be alone. *We created the human, and we know what [s]he whispers to [her]self. We are closer to [her] than [her] jugular vein* (50:16, Quran). I did not need a go-between telling me what God thinks. Not once did I feel that Islam was incompatible with my lesbian identity. Of course, Satan tries his best to make me think otherwise. I know this because again God has told me about Satan:

When you read the Quran, you shall seek refuge in

God from Satan the rejected (16:98).

He has no power over those who believe and trust in
their Lord (16:99).

Not once did I entertain thoughts of abandoning Islam or my sexuality. I did feel isolated, however, since my family did not share
my affirming perspective about Islam and sexuality. But my iman
(faith) counteracted my isolation and it allowed me to connect with
like-minded individuals.

Islam is not a static and monolithic entity as many people (non-
Muslims and Muslims) believe. Reducing Islam to a monolithic
entity is confirming orientalist constructions of Islam and Muslims,
and erases its diversity and plurality. Said's[4] (1978) work on orientalism warns us against reducing Islam to any one thing. Islam is
dynamic and it is practiced in many ways.

Growing up I was taught that there is one *right* way to practice
Islam and be as a Muslim. I have been taught that the *right* way to
be Muslim is the Sunni tradition. It was not until I was in school
that I was exposed to other ways of practising Islam from my Shia,
Sufi, Ahmadiyya, and Ismaili friends. I realized that I had a limited
knowledge about God, Islam, and Muslims and needed to engage
in doing my own study and reflection (ijtihad). Ijtihad is about
deploying one's spirit, experiences, intellect, emotion and body in
understanding faith-related matters.

Islam means different things to people and I can only talk
about my Islam. Determining the meaning of anything requires
an understanding of the politics of knowledge generation and the
role language plays among other things. Knowledge is socially
constructed and is a reflection of the producer's ideologies, experiences, and belief systems. For instance, ideas about inferiority
are interwoven with notions of race, gender, ability, and sexuality.
The orientalist constructions of the South Asian woman in "need
of saving" from their oppressive religion, culture, and so on is still
thriving in the minds of people. As Mohanty[5] (2002) tells us:

> (S)cholars often locate "third world women" in terms
> of the underdevelopment, oppressive traditions, high
> illiteracy, rural and urban poverty, religious fanati-
> cism, and "overpopulation" of particular Asian,
> African, Middle Eastern, and Latin American coun-
> tries . . . Besides being normed on a white, Western
> (read progressive/modern)/ non-Western (read back-
> ward/traditional) hierarchy, these analyses freeze third
> world women in time, space, and history (p. 196).

Therefore we have to ask ourselves who was and is in charge
of knowledge production around the meaning of Islam? The discourse around *submitting* and *submission* leaves out the agency of
the person engaging in the act of submitting and submission. How
is that individual conceptualized in this equation? God urges us
to *reflect*, not to follow blindly. God poses intelligible arguments
to engage the reader and to invite them to choose their faith. For
instance, in the Bible (Job: 38-42, New King James Version) God
asks Prophet Job (Ayyub) the following questions:

> Who is this who darkens counsel By words without
> knowledge?

> Now prepare yourself like a man; I will question you,
> and you shall answer Me.

> Where were you when I laid the foundations of the
> earth? Tell Me, if you have understanding. Who
> determined its measurements? Surely you know! Or
> who stretched the line upon it? To what were its foun-
> dations fastened? Or who laid its cornerstone . . . (Job
> 38:1-6, New King James Version Bible).

My Islam is about choice, deploying one's agency with an
emphasis on action and engaging in continuous ijtihad. It is about
trust, engagement with giving yourself over to a higher power with
your whole being. It is having the freedom and using it. It is giving

myself wholeheartedly over to the Creator out of choice and desire.

One of the best things about growing up in Greater Toronto is that you are blessed with the opportunity to engage in relationships with individuals who identify themselves as Rastas, Jews, Hindus, Christians, Buddhists, Atheists, Agnostic, and Wiccan among others. From all these relationships, I learned different ways of relating to God and as a result my relationship with God shifted over the years and continues to do so. I have had to answer why I believe as I do. I had to return to the Quran to unpack the basic tenets of Islam so that I could conduct dawa proper. I was becoming an informed Muslim.

I was blessed to be able to attend the Sunday worship services at Metropolitan Community Church of Toronto (MCCT) where religious queers and allies can collectively worship God. MCCT welcomes congregants from all faith traditions and is spearheaded by Sr Pastor, Reverend Dr Brent Hawkes. My family and Muslim friends were disconcerted about my involvement with Christianity and the Church. *You were thinking of volunteering where? Church? Why?* On various occasions my sister teased and asked me outright if I had converted. What if I did convert to Christianity? Would I be forbidden from my family's gatherings and home? These questions drew grave silence.

An old queer Muslim friend advised me that my prayers were not accepted when I worshipped at the Church. I was flabbergasted. Other friends have shared similar views. Does worshipping at Church classify me as an *unauthentic* Muslim? Did we all forget the many stories of Muslims seeking asylum with non-Muslims? Of people offering Muslims worship spaces and protection in North America? There are countless examples in the Bible and Quran about people of the scripture helping one another.

One of my biggest objectives is to foster a friendship with God, who is Wali. My attitude changed from: "If I don't do this or that this way for a certain number of times, I'll be sent to Hell." My thinking about God shifted to: "God wants me to succeed and win." It went from *fearing God* to *respecting* and *understanding* God. I befriended God and the *fearing* changed to reorienting myself to God's infinite mercies and compassion.

Muslim Women

Muslim women and their bodies are subjected to various discourses which almost always centralize their marginality. The topic of hijab or veiling is where most often the marginality of Muslim women is constructed and debated, regardless of the fact that the hijab serves various functions and is contingent on the woman's application. I believe that whether to wear a hijab or a head cover should be solely the wearer's choice. Of course "choice" is at times an illusion since the decision could already be made for us in one way or another. I would say that if wearing the hijab makes you happy, feel empowered, and doesn't hurt anyone then go for it.

Marriage is yet another contested socially constructed concept. Marriage is not for everyone, and it should be defined by the individuals deciding to get married. Often it is the state, religion, and society at large telling us what a marriage should be. Marriage often gets constructed as the panacea for satisfying sexual urges. You get married to regulate your life and sexuality, have children and maintain a certain way of living. This formula works for some Muslims and not for others.

Many Muslims will place the Sharia, hadith, and fatwas in the same bracket as the Quran. But Quran is the word of God, the others are not. The Sharia is a compilation of what jurists in Islam have interpreted God's covenant and scripture to mean. The Sharia laws are products of cultural, political and historical factors that are androcentric, heterosexist and ableist. Very few imams will be honest in admitting this. Certain verses in the Quran are deployed to justify the use of hadith and sunna as gospel. These verses are quoted in isolation from their historical, cultural, and sociopolitical contexts.

In the Bible and Quran, all of God's messengers and prophets constantly remind us that they merely are the vehicles to bring God's message (17:59, Quran). There is intense debate in the various sects in Islam on where and when the prophet Muhammed said what, and what are the authentic hadith and so on. If God wanted us to follow anyone other than God then it would have been noted in the scripture. Why not follow God's sunna, who is our Lord and Saviour?

> Such is the sunna of God for those who have passed on before. You will find that there is no substitute for the sunna of God (33:62).

> Shall I seek other than God as a source of law, when [God] He has revealed to you this book fully detailed? (6:114-115).

Diversity Within Muslims

"Muslim" and "lesbian" are often seen as antithetical identity.[6] This is discouraging for people like myself. The literature also shows that queer individuals are often forced to choose between their sexual and religious identities due to the normative understandings of Islam (Yip[7], 2005). Islamic history and culture are filled with countless examples of same-sex relationships, and gender variance (Habib, 2007a[8], 2007b[9]; Rahman, 2014[10]). The rationale offered to support the notion of Islam's incompatibility with sexually and gender diverse identities is found in certain verses in the Quran. These verses are found mainly in the story of Prophet Lut (Lot), where the destruction of his community is seen as a result of homoerotic engagement between males (Kugle[11], 2010). A queer reading of the Quran will elucidate the political, social, cultural, and androcentric ideas embedded in the scripture.

Existing as the *other* within society and as someone who subscribes to queer politics, I have an investment in upsetting traditional hetero- and homo-norms. Kugle (2010) appositely identifies that queer Muslims approach the Quranic scripture with "resistance and renewal" (p. 40). In resistance, the aim is to critically query any previous interpretations of Prophet Lut's story and all other Quranic verses that are employed to condemn same-sex relationships. The concept of renewal allows queer Muslims to emphasize parts of the scripture that celebrates diversity in all its forms. Again, there is no word in the Quranic scripture that refers to homosexuality (Kugle, 2010).

God is free from error and humans are not. Humans can and have made mistakes in translating the word of God. Not all translations of the Quran are the same, and there is no one true interpretation of the Quran. Language is forever shifting and is contingent on the meanings we attach to it. We do not exist outside language. Only God has dominion over truth, and human interpretations are mere hypothetical guesses about *the truth*. More often than not, Islamic scholars fail to account for their heteronormative cis-privilege when interpreting and translating the Quranic holy scriptures. They fail to consider that there is another reason behind the destruction of Sodom and Gomorrah. For instance, rejecting the word of God.

Approaches to the Quranic scriptures from queer and feminist perspectives reinterpret the controversial verses (Jamal[12], 2001; Kugle[13], 2003) by *queering* the Quran and its understandings and practice in contemporary society to expose cultural and patriarchal influences.

I took my Muslim identity and iman (faith) for granted prior to critically reflecting on the discussions I had with my friends and family on the compatibility of Islam and non-heterosexual identities. I now realize that I am Muslim by choice and not because I was born into a Muslim household. This was a huge shift in my perspective as the majority of the queer Muslims I met had to abandon either Islam or their queer identity. The notion that being queer is a test from God is an overused trope in queer Muslim circles. God can deploy any means to test our iman. I find it problematic to concentrate solely on one's queer status as a test from God. God can test us on the basis of wealth, disease, poverty and so forth.

Identifying as a lesbian has brought me closer to God, and has strengthened my iman. When the people I cared about and loved deeply failed to embrace, let alone entertain, my perspective on Islam and sexuality, I was led to critically reflect on what it meant to be a lesbian Muslim. I had to re-read, re-examine and re-configure the Quranic scripture, and to this day I remain steadfast in my belief that being queer and Muslim is not an oxymoron. Iman and ijtihad are important in considering the predicament so many queer Muslims find themselves in. We forget that it was God who deposited love into our parents' hearts so that they could care for us. It is God's love and approval we need to seek more than any other relationship.

Conclusion

There are many ways of practicing Islam. When we deviate from prescribed norms we create tensions that push us toward the unknown. I find myself traversing between inherited identities and social processes shaped by colonial and imperial histories, and I continuously have to negotiate ways to resist such influences. The subject position that I occupy is of resistance in order to shape and create new realities. It is due to God's infinite mercies that I have managed to overcome adversities. We should not allow parents, imams, significant others, siblings and others to take away our agency, and dictate or sever our relationship with God. I conclude with a shortened version of the Serenity Prayer:

> God grant me the serenity to accept the things I
> cannot change, courage to change the things I can,
> and wisdom to know the difference. Amen/Ameen.

Notes

1. Centralizing women's narratives verses the 'his-story' in history.

2. Using lower caps purposefully since this term is sensationalized.

3. bell hooks, *Talking Back: Thinking Feminist, Thinking Black*. (New York: Routledge, 2015).

4. Edward W Said, *Orientalism*. (New York: Vintage Books Edition, 1978).

5. Chandra T Mohanty, "Cartographies of struggle: Third world women and the politics of feminism," in *Race critical theories: Text and context*, ed. P Essed & DT Goldberg. (Oxford: Blackwell Publishers, 2002), 195-219.

6. Asifa Siraj, "Isolated, invisible, and in the closet: The life story of a Scottish Muslim lesbian," *Journal of Lesbian Studies, 15*(1) (2011): 99-121.

7. Andrew KT Yip. "Queering religious texts: An exploration of British non-heterosexual Christians' and Muslims' strategy of constructing sexuality affirming hermeneutics," *Sociology, 39*(1) (2005): 47-65. doi:10.1177/0038038505049000

8. Samar Habib, *Female homosexuality in the Middle East: histories and representations*. (New York: Routledge, 2007).

9. Samar Habib, "Reading the familiarity of the past: An introduction to medieval Arabic literature on female homosexuality," *EnterText, 7*(2) (2007): 162-172.

10. Momin Rahman, *Homosexualities, Muslim cultures and modernity*. (Basingstoke: Palgrave Macmillan, 2014).

11. Scott Alan Kugle, *Homosexuality in Islam: Critical reflection on gay, lesbian, and transgender Muslims*. (Oxford: OneWorld, 2010).

12. Amreen Jamal, "The story of Lot and the Quran's perception of the morality of same-sex sexuality," *Journal of Homosexuality, 41*(1) (2001): 1-88. doi:10.1300/J082v41n01_01

13. Scott Alan Kugle, "Sexuality, diversity and ethics in the agenda of progressive Muslims" in *Progressive Muslims: On justice, gender, and pluralism*, ed. O Safi. (Oxford: Oneworld, 2003), 190-234.

Not so Black and White

HANAN ABDULMALIK

THAT'S HOW MY life in Toronto started: determined to not like Canada. I had already found a home. I loved England. I loved London. I loved Sussex. There was no room for more. It was my first summer in Toronto, and I spent the summer aimlessly riding the subway from East to West, and then from North to South, and back again. I started choosing random subway stations to get off and explore. I discovered the North York Central library, different parts of Yonge Street, the Indy coffee shops, and the amazing food and sounds of Harbourfront in the summer.

I allowed myself to look around, notice, listen, and smell Toronto. It was a lonely experience, but a fascinating one. As the summer wore on, I missed my friends dearly but slowly came to terms with the idea of staying here. Staying in England was not an option. We were immigrating to Canada, to settle in Toronto. I was not happy with the idea but by the end of the summer, I knew that I was going to be okay.

I was born in Ethiopia, where coffee was born. Coffee and I relate a lot. When I reflect upon the "who am I" identity, I'm drawn to think again about coffee. How wonderfully grown-up it has become; who would have ever thought that coffee would become intrinsically Canadian, accepted and celebrated coast to coast—the idea that perhaps it comes from somewhere seems less important to what it has become, and so I continue with my story.

My ancestors stem from a city called Harar—an ancient walled city in the eastern part of Ethiopia on a plateau with deep gorges surrounded by deserts and savannah. There are over eighty ethnic groups and just as many languages spoken in Ethiopia. The tiny city-state within Ethiopia named Harar is called "Gey" by its inhabitants and that literally means "the City." Its people—an assortment of different tribes—simply refer to themselves as "gey usu," a neutral phrase meaning city-dwellers. Harari identity does not lie on ethnicity, but rather on a multicultural reality with a common shared value and faith. Once in touch with Harari people, staying or becoming Harari is relatively simple—again, coffee can be from anywhere near the equator, but after it is grown and harvested, dried and cleaned, coffee goes around the world and becomes the coffee requested for the world over.

I was twelve when my parents decided to move the family out of Ethiopia. The Ethiopian government at the time had decided to enforce mandatory military service by drafting young men from schools, markets, farms, and streets. To avoid the draft, families kept young men at home, away from schools and streets. There was a tangible sense of unease, as people grew increasingly discontent with the government. My father ran a burgeoning business and did not want to leave that behind, but he decided it was time to move his family to a secure country until the political situation in Ethiopia improved. Cairo, Egypt seemed like the perfect choice as it was a thriving multicultural cosmopolitan hub. As my family and I boarded a plane to Cairo, unsure of what the future held, the year was 1985 and it felt like that exit from Ethiopia changed all of our lives forever.

My parents have always been filled with high hopes and expectations for each one of their children. Living in Egypt meant that we were going to be totally immersed in Egyptian Arabic culture, study religion, and excel in school. As we settled into our new life in Cairo, my parents had to make some difficult choices regarding schooling for my siblings and I. It was important for them that we learned Arabic and studied religion, and it was equally as important to them that we received a western standard education. The schooling choices presented then appear now to be some kind of dichotomy: a schooling curriculum that focused on preparing children for success in the world (*dunya*, the temporal world) and its earthly concerns and possessions, or a curriculum that prepared us for the afterlife (*akhirah*, meaning the end). The ideal school that they had dreamt up would recognize *dunya* and *akhirah* as two inseparable dimensions of the same basic reality of a life of submission, and would therefore provide the highest level of Islamic education as well as implement the *British* curriculum. Such a school did not exist, however, and we ended up enrolled in a British school, studying the British curriculum, supplemented with an Arabic teacher who came to the house twice a week to teach us Arabic.

As the political situation in Ethiopia improved, it was time for our next move. My parents decided to move the younger kids back to Ethiopia, and at the age of fifteen, for reasons that I could not comprehend, I was to continue my British education in a boarding school in the village of Upper Dicker in Southern England. The school was set in 140 acres of Sussex Downs in an area of outstanding natural beauty. I landed at Gatwick airport and, accompanied by my father and older brother, boarded a train to take me to the boarding school where I was to spend two years of my life. We arrived there to be greeted by the headmaster and the woman in charge of the "house" where I would be living. It was both exhilarating and confusing at the same time. I come from a tight-knit family, in which decisions had always been made for me, and all of a sudden, an hour into arrival, after small talk with the headmaster and a tour of the school and its boarding facilities, my father was going to walk away and leave me there in charge of my own destiny and therefore my own identity? It felt unfathomable but that's exactly what happened.

I walked timidly into my new bedroom, and met my two room-mates who had just flown in from Japan and Germany respectively. The bell rang, we congregated in the corridors for roll call, the housemistress called out the name of each kid in that corridor, and as we all looked at each other and replied "present" when our names were called, I knew deep in my heart that I was going to be okay. I was going to love this boarding school and love England. And love them I did.

In many ways boarding school was a microcosm of life in a major Canadian city: the school was filled with children from all over the world. At the end of my two years I knew I wanted to stay in England forever. I had friends from all over the world, I felt like I had found myself, multiculturalism and diversity were important to me, and I was comfortable with who I had become. The decision to stay, however, was not destined to be mine to make. University was expensive in England for an alien on a student's visa. I had a lot of family that had immigrated to Toronto by this point. Canada was calling, and I was resisting. I reached a compromise with my family and agreed to give Toronto a chance by checking it out for the summer.

I eventually started school at the University of Toronto. I chose the Mississauga campus because it was a smaller campus, and that would suit me better. In my first week of school, I quickly got introduced to the identity politics that frames much of life in North America. Should I join the Black Students Association? How do you define Blackness? I knew I was black but race as an identity was completely foreign to me. In North America, and in the West in general, race is based upon a dichotomous understanding where Black and White are opposites.

In Ethiopia the many different languages and cultures provided deep-rooted meaning and ties to the land and people, and my understanding of identity did not exist in the realm of opposites.

What did I have in common with the black students with whom I

did not share much beyond what felt like the singularly most important identifier of race? Similarly I struggled with the idea of joining
the Muslim Students Association, which could have been renamed
the Indo-Pakistani Association without anyone really noticing.
There was no one who looked like me. Would I belong if I didn't
cover my hair? It was the first time that I had been forced to look
at myself vis-à-vis singular versions of identity, and I've since been
fascinated with expressions of identity both perceived and imposed.

Fast forward a few years and I found myself in Sudan, navigat-
ing a different set of questions related to identity. What does it
mean to be Arab? What does it mean to be African? The year was
2005, many years before the secession of South Sudan. Southern
Sudan and North Sudan were on the verge of signing a historic
peace agreement after fifty years of civil war. As part of the peace
agreement, the warring parties were to sit together in parliament to
enact laws to run the new united country. The Canadian government had committed to providing legislative development support
during this important time, and I was part of the implementation
team. During the needs assessment phase, I made plans to attend a
training session that was being provided to the top 100 commanders of the Southern People's Liberation Movement (SPLM). These
commanders were all likely to be nominated to influential government posts or parliament upon the signing of the peace agreement.

Travel to South Sudan was long and tedious. I flew via Nairobi
to Lokichiggio airport, which had been established as a relief base
for South Sudan. Upon arrival at this airport, located thirty kilo-
meters away from the international border with South Sudan, I,
along with a couple of passengers—taking with us lots of bottled
water, cooking gas, eggs, and various other food items—boarded a
small plane to make the trip into South Sudan. I arrived at the training location to be warmly greeted by the host who had extended
the invitation, but as I looked around I noticed many commanders
pointing at me as they whispered to each other.

A few minutes later some of the men walked over and started

asking questions: What was I doing there? Where was I from? Why did I come? Passport still in hand, I waved it up high, and stated proudly that I was Canadian, and went on to explain that I was there on Canadian business to assess the kind of legislative support that we may be able to provide upon the signing of the peace agreement. They were not satisfied with my answer and the questions continued. Where was I really from? Who sent me? Was I North Sudanese? Was I a North Sudanese Arab spy?

Here I was, an Ethiopian Canadian in a remote area of South Sudan where there were no telephones or electricity, there was no easy way out, and I was being accused of being a Northern Sudanese Arab spy, because apparently I looked like a North Sudanese "Arab"! Luckily, most of the members of the SPLM had spent time in Ethiopia in exile and spoke Amharic. When I explained that I was Ethiopian by birth, they verified that by testing my language skills. I was suddenly given the warmest greetings: I was their long-lost African sister.

This year I celebrate the twenty-fifth anniversary of my immigration to Canada. I have the privilege to be married to my good friend, husband, father to my kids, and hundred percent fellow coffee enthusiast and confidante. His name suggests that he is a Canadian of Irish descent—his looks suggest that he is what is frequently called "white." The longer I stay in Canada, especially as we interact with the school system through my kids, the more of a nuanced understanding I have of what it means to be black and white in Canada, and what it means to be a Muslim in Canada. I no longer worry about how people identify me, and the associated stereotypes. I have accepted that my identity shifts, depending on where I am, and what I am doing.

When people ask my two daughters where they are from, they often list all the countries they have travelled to and love: always starting with Canada and Ethiopia, and quickly followed by Cuba, France, Emirates, and India. We think this is amazing. When my grandmother met my husband for the first time on our first trip together to Ethiopia, we anxiously awaited her reaction to meeting this foreign man. She responded with, "Where is the foreigner that you're talking about? He is one of us! Serve him coffee!"

I enjoy coffee when prepared in the simplest traditional way. Green beans roasted on a flat pan, the pungent smell filling the air as the coffee beans slowly turn black. Roasted beans are ground and stirred into a clay pot or "jebena" with some water, and cooked slowly until the steam begins to spout. Before pouring it, the coffee is set aside and the grounds allowed to settle at the bottom, so that the brew rises to the top.

This is a tradition that I have carried with me and enjoy with family and friends several times a week. In very much the same way, in becoming Canadian I find that I have continued the traditions of my ancestors: membership in a society that is based on shared space, shared values, common language, and a fundamental respect for diversity.

Five Bucks

LINA KHATIB

THE WINDOWS OF our silver Dodge van shattered as we crashed into a snow bank on the side of the highway. I was one month old, travelling from Calgary to Toronto with my family. Earlier, my parents had loaded the van that afternoon with a few pots and pans, a box of clothing, a fan, landed immigrant papers, and five kids under the age of eight. My mother had wrapped me in a blanket and placed me inside a basket that wobbled on my seven-year-old sister's lap as my father drove down the TransCanada highway.

"She looks like baby Moses," my six-year-old brother exclaimed. "Maybe we should put her into a river so that we could have more space in the van!"

The snowstorm hit hard that evening. My father lost control of the van and it rolled over twice before landing into a snow bank. I flew out of my basket into the air but miraculously landed back into my sister's little arms. To this day, she insists that she is to thank for saving my life. No one was seriously injured; two of my siblings had a few minor cuts from the broken glass. My brother always liked to chant "faster, faster," whenever we drove down a highway in hopes that the car might spin out of control and crash into something. Now he hid his cold face in my mother's arm, his boots sunk in the white snow beside the highway. Stranded and shivering, my family waited to be picked up by a tow truck.

We all stayed in a motel room that night. My father used up his little cash to spend on our room and repairing the van. When he returned from the body shop, he took out a crumpled five-dollar bill from his wallet and handed it to my mother. Without a word, she walked to a nearby convenience store and brought back supplies—a jug of milk and packet of Wonder Bread. We took turns chugging from the jug. My mother repeatedly insisted my father take a sip, but he shook his head as he gazed out the small window.

My parents opted to live in Calgary when they arrived in Canada because they had close friends living there. We left for Toronto only a few weeks later because it was the only city offering the Kaplan Course that my mother needed to update her foreign medical credentials. Despite challenges, they were grateful to have made it to Canada, far away from the terror of the Assad regime in Syria.

My parents came from middle-class Syrian families. My paternal grandfather was a school teacher and my maternal grandfather was a bureaucrat who made his fortune growing cotton. They lived in a beautiful villa in Aleppo, with a large balcony, surrounded by fragrant jasmine flowers, and protected by iron gates.

My mother grew up with four brothers and nurtured high ambitions. She studied medicine and was destined to become the head doctor at the largest hospital in Aleppo. My father was the oldest son in his family and a spirited man with strong convictions. He had little patience for routine life and disliked the rigid structure of school and authority. Contrary to his parents' wishes, he dropped out of the engineering program at university. He was a man with a thousand friends and a remarkable ability to gather and mobilize people around causes that mattered to him.

When my parents met in university, the Ba'ath party was ruling the country under the dictatorship of Hafez Al-Assad. The middle class in Syria was slowly diminishing, and although Syria was not a poor country, it was certainly corrupt. The kind of honest business that once made my grandfather a wealthy man was a rarity. It was a known fact that anyone who held a high position in government or in the military must have taken or received bribes. Times were changing as the rich got richer and the poor got poorer.

My mother fell in love with my father's adventurous spirit and high ideals. He encouraged her to join a popular youth movement that wished to overthrow the government and establish a freer and fairer Syria. This endeavour and their love affair was contrary to her parents' wishes. They wanted to see my mother graduate with high distinction and to stay out of politics.

The Mukhabarat, or the secret police, infested the streets of Syria. They once came banging at my grandfather's door looking for my mother. My grandfather was a tall, well-built man with a long face and stern eyes. He opened the door slightly, when three officers pushed him aside and marched inside. They wanted to find out about my mother. The Mukhabarat could arrest anyone and throw them into prison. As the political situation became worse and the opposition movement grew, disappearances became more and more common. The victims often had nothing to do with politics and were merely associated with someone who was known to oppose the government. In prison people were tortured and often forced to confess to crimes they did not commit. My grandfather later told my mother that he would have rather seen her die than have her home that evening, because being dead was better than being in the hands of the Mukhabarat.

Despite this culture of fear and censorship, my father's invitation to meet with the revolutionaries made my mother's eyes glitter with purpose. My parents spent the daytime working and the night hours meeting in secret locations, recruiting new members and forming alliances. Eventually, my grandparents gave in and allowed my mother to marry my father. Soon my mother announced her pregnancy. Unfortunately, the joyful anticipation of the first born was quickly broken when my father was dragged away from a friend's home and taken to the notorious Kafarsuseh prison. The first time my father saw his first born was in prison and only for a few minutes. She was eleven months old, a few weeks away from taking her first steps. My father said goodbye to his wife and daughter, knowing that they might never see him again.

My father's name was on a list of seventeen prisoners sentenced to death. He was to be executed in a matter of days. A miraculous twist altered this fate when a conscionable prison guard offered to help the death row prisoners to escape. He staged a medical emergency and unlocked the prison gates, and the seventeen men piled into the back of an ambulance vehicle. My father was fortunate. Many political prisoners never returned home to their families. Some received the mercy of hanging, while others were left to rot and die a slow death in prison.

My father immediately fled to neighbouring Jordan, where he secretly arranged to meet my mother. While they were on the run, my father received the sad news of his father's death. When the Mukhabarat could not find my father, they went after his father. They barged into my grandfather's home in the middle of the night to question him. My grandfather had no idea where my father was. No matter how many times he repeated this truth, their thirst for vengeance was not quenched. After hours of brutal interrogation, they shoved him outside his house in his pajamas and shot him execution style.

When my parents left Syria, they never imagined that thirty-five years would pass without them stepping foot back in their homeland. In 1982, a few years after they left, the town of Hama was besieged for twenty-seven days. The Syrian army murdered over 30,000 thousand people and the town's infrastructure was completely destroyed. The massacre effectively ended the campaign against the Syrian government. The Syrian people were silenced.

Hafez Al-Assad died in 2000. My parents had hope that his western-educated son, Bashar, would rule with more compassion. They even dreamt that they might be able to visit Syria. I watched the news of Al-Assad's death on satellite television at home and still remember my parents' sense of hope funneling into my heart. Alas, it would take the Syrian people eleven years and the encouragement of surrounding countries like Tunisia and Egypt to stand up against Bashar, who like his father is a vicious dictator and a war criminal.

I joined my family at The Toronto Film Festival in 2014 to watch a documentary called *Silvered Water* about the modern Syrian revolution. My husband covered my eyes with his hands as the scenes of torture and abuse became more graphic, but I peeled his hands from my moistened eyes and continued watching. I had to know. I had to be angry. Alongside the hideous scenes of the war were scenes of honour and heroism. Little children dodging bullets and men dragging dead bodies from the streets. As I watched, I rubbed my pregnant belly and prayed that the producer of the documentary would spare me from images of children being hurt. What we dreaded most became a horrific reality and there was now more blood on Bashar Al-Assad's hands than there was on his notorious father's.

The Canadian government rescued my family in the late 1980s and gave us a peaceful place to call home. My father loves Canada. It is the first place in the world that allowed him not only to speak openly about his views, but also to participate freely in politics. He regularly invites politicians of different backgrounds to his home for information sessions. He has been encouraging me to join a political party and to vote since the day I turned eighteen.

I was born in Calgary and raised in Toronto; I have never been to Syria. Given that the ruling party that imprisoned my father continues to rule today, it is nearly impossible for me to safely visit my home country. It never bothered me much when I was younger, because deep down I always believed I would eventually visit and see all of the beautiful sites that my parents reminisced about. The medieval buildings in Aleppo, Al-Madina Souq, the Great Mosque and Citadel of Aleppo and the neighbourhoods in which my parents grew up. Sadly, all of these sites have been damaged or destroyed as a result of the current war in Syria. This is a loss I mourn deeply.

I have always been proud of being a Canadian Syrian. Growing up in the Toronto public school system, I learned to appreciate other cultures and religions. I remember preparing a bowl of hummus and colouring a large poster of the Syrian flag so that I could have something to present in my grade four class on heritage day. The classroom was splashed with bright colours as students proudly presented their cultural dresses, foods, and posters. I eagerly explained to my classmates that I was from Aleppo, and that the best pistachios came from my region.

Today as I look at my newborn, I see that he has my husband's slanted Bengali eyes, my wavy hair, and a mix of our complexions, and I wonder what his classroom will be like when he starts kindergarten. Will he be proud of where his grandparents came from? Will he know his family's struggles that brought him where he is today? Will he understand the blessing of being Canadian? My son symbolizes the unity of peace, acceptance, and love that my family found when they arrived in Canada.

As a first generation Muslim Arab who wears a hijab, I find the journey to self-discovery and understanding identity to be a complex one. I never felt weak when a boy in grade eight mocked me by wearing a piece of paper on his head. He got little attention for it, because none of my classmates thought it was funny. On September 11, 2001, my entire high school watched the Twin Towers crumble on the television screen in the school library, and I watched with them without ever feeling the need to apologize for the actions of people who were so-called Muslims, because I, in no way, related to them. My mother carefully surrounded me with mentors and friends I could relate to.

Nonetheless, I was a shy child and wanted nothing more than to blend into my surroundings like a blade of grass in a field. My high school history teacher once called me out in class and asked me what Islam taught about the topic of knowledge. The entire class turned to face me and I wanted to melt into my seat as my face flashed red. I shrugged my shoulders and said, "I don't know" in a desperate attempt to get the spotlight off me. I understood why he chose to single me out, but I also despised him for doing so. On the bus ride home that day, I thought of the word "read"—which was the first word of the Quran revealed to the Prophet Muhammad from God. I thought of the answers I could have given my teacher and I wanted to kick myself for the lost opportunity.

During my first year at university, in my political science class, I felt that religion had become an insult to reason and logic. Denying that, according to many of my professors and classmates, would put me in the category of Pre-Enlightenment. It was difficult to reconcile what I was learning in class with the beliefs that I was brought up with. Nonetheless, I was done being a fly on the wall. I hated the idea that others could assume that my perspective was based on my outer appearance. When lively discussions sparked in my tutorials, I would make it a point to raise my hand and state my opinions. I felt a great desire to differentiate myself as an individual and to be heard.

In my third year, I went to complete a semester abroad in France. I was determined to mingle with as many different types of people as possible. Among my group of friends were a few French students originally from Algeria. I enjoyed political discussions with them, but got frustrated when one of the guys, Omar, insisted that Saudi Arabia was the best country in the world. "Saudi Arabia is one of the few Islamic countries left in the world," he said. "I hope to finish my studies and live there one day."

I told him, "Saudi Arabia is posing as an Islamic State and is actually filled with hypocrisy and contradictions. For God's sake, Canada is more of an Islamic country than Saudi Arabia!"

Omar lifted his eyebrows in disbelief. "Canada has very few bearded men and veiled women, how could you compare it to an Islamic country?"

"That is so narrow-minded of you," I shot back. "Not every city in Canada has a masjid or halal meat shops, but the Canadian Charter of Rights and Freedoms in many ways is a reflection of the

Islamic principles taught to us by the Prophet Muhammad, peace be upon him. For instance, in Islam, human beings are all equal before God, just as in Canada all citizens are equal before the law."

No matter how many examples I gave Omar, he would not agree with me. At the time, I pitied his simplistic view of the world and of Islam. Today, I regret my youthful pride and frustration, and I am glad that we had that discussion. It helped me define my Islam and the way I wanted to practice it. I realized later that I loved my faith just as much as he did, but that given our different contexts, we viewed the practice of Islam differently and it was important for me to accept that.

There are some experiences I have had as a Muslim woman in Canada that I still do not know how to accept. In my second year at university, I interned with a Member of Parliament in Ottawa. I was often asked to sit in at committee meetings and take notes. One afternoon, as I sat in at a meeting, I could not help noticing one of the MPs staring at me from across the room. He was a tall Caucasian man with white hair. Once the meeting was over, he walked over to where I was sitting.

"Excuse me, are you that woman from that TV show *Mosque on the Prairie?*" he asked with a wide smile on his face.

"Uh . . . no," I replied.

He walked away without another word. I could not believe that he would ask me such a question. He was supposedly an educated man. Was I possibly the only woman he had ever seen wearing a hjiab aside from the character on that TV show? I wanted so much to have responded by asking if he was the man from the TV show *Corner Gas*.

When I started my masters in public administration at Queen's University in Kingston, Ontario, I knew it would be a challenging time. I was the only Muslim student in the entire program and the burden of representation weighed heavily on me. I was used to people asking me why I wore hijab and if I would have an arranged marriage. To my surprise, it ended up being an uneventful time and

I moved on to work for the Ontario Public Service where Muslim women in hijab are also a rarity. I now have a sense of satisfaction in having studied and worked in places where you would not normally find a Muslim woman.

I am fortunate to have had the opportunity to reflect on my life. My siblings and I now live privileged lives where we can turn up our noses at the idea of eating white Wonder Bread. My parents spent many years desperately trying to keep their heads above water, asking each other questions like: Where will we live? What will the children eat? Is it safe to leave our home?

When they describe our family's early years, the song by Charles Aznavour, "La Bohéme," comes to mind. I heard my parents listening to it recently on YouTube. I was surprised to hear them enjoying western music, let alone a French song. It turns out that he was very popular in Syria in the 60s and my parents were big fans. The song tells the story of a painter who recalls his artistic life as a young man and how he was hungry but still happy. While my parents tell us about our own early days in Canada, how they too were hungry but happy, I know that they were the most trying years of their lives.

For Better or For Worse

GHAZIA SIRTAJ

When I was a child, I saw God, I saw angels; I
watched the mysteries of the higher and lower worlds.
I thought all men saw the same. At last I realized that
they did not see. — SHAMS TABRIZ

I WAS BORN AND raised in Karachi, Pakistan. My father (Pa)
named me Ghazia, derived from "ghazi," which means "war-
rior" in Arabic. My family consisted of Pa, my stepmother, my
elder stepsister, myself, and my younger brother whom I call Bhai.
My story begins in 2002 when I got married within six hours of
meeting my husband in Karachi; he was travelling back to Canada
the next morning.

2002

My husband (H) gave me Quranic verses and hadith to read about
how women are prohibited to wear perfume and do personal
grooming in Islam. He and his family criticized my dressing as non-
Islamic and wanted me to wear hijab, abayah, and shoes of certain
colours. They wanted our wedding reception to be segregated. My
mother-in-law (MIL) did not want a professional photographer,

saying it was un-Islamic. Pa refused to hold the reception in the US, where my in-laws lived, but instead gave me cash. MIL told me to ask Pa for money instead of any dowry. It is not uncommon for in-laws to make such demands in Pakistan.

I admired Pa's commitment towards his second wife. Pa had divorced my mother. Coming from such a background, I wanted to be a respectful wife and daughter-in-law; I would wish my in-laws on their birthdays, offered to cook and help around the house during my visits, and connected with my in-laws in North America.

2003

Before moving to Canada, I shared my concerns with H about his mood swings and unpredictable anger, I suggested we end the marriage. Obviously I was not the girl he desired for a wife. He said I felt that only because my stepsister was going through a divorce. He would visit for four days for the reception and then I would go with him to Canada.

H was resentful and distant and shared no physical intimacy even when we were living together, calling me unattractive, without a dressing sense. I tried new recipes and different dishes for him, which irritated him. If I tried to prepare his clothes for work he accused me of dictating terms and changing his dressing style.

There were regular inquiries about pregnancy from his family and cousins willingly suggesting effective positions to conceive.

Once, H went to drop a friend at the airport and I happened to read his emails. I found emails from women with whom he was having affairs. And he had seemed so religious! I questioned him, and he said they were not a big deal, such things happened after living in North America. I asked if the same rule applied to me. This infuriated him and he pinned me down to the bed and sat on me, pressing his knees on my chest. After that day I was neither allowed to shop nor do groceries on my own. If I bought something he returned it, saying it was against Islam or unaffordable.

Personal grooming was not allowed and I was forbidden to have rice, soda, chocolates, ice cream, cookies, whole milk, and more than 1 slice of bread for breakfast.

Dining out and movies were haram, a cellphone was an unaffordable expense; every month he complained about bills, and when I offered to work, he argued that that would take the Bara'kah away from the house. Also, if a woman worked she was sexually harassed by employers. When I wanted to study, I was told education was expensive.

2004

The abuse continued. I was called names for wearing perfume and going against Allah. He would stop eating or talking with me. I spent nights standing by the nightstand crying.

When I asked to study he said that taxes would increase because of education, and if I suggested university scholarships and student loans, he said there were none, or he would have completed his masters. I was not allowed to drive.

I spoke to his mother and sisters, but they offered no help.

2005 - 2006

We performed Hajj and during the entire pilgrimage he called me a disgrace to womanhood for bringing out the worst in him and told me Allah's wrath would fall on me. I was allowed to visit Pakistan after Hajj and was able to disclose my problems to my family. Pa's wife said that respectable daughters did not disgrace their families with divorce. I discussed the abuse with H's family and was advised to not go back, but not disclose my reasons to anyone.

Pa enrolled me in French classes at Alliance Française. After completing the course I returned. A neighbour told me that a Russian woman had visited my apartment a few times while I was away. I thought it was one of H's colleagues and asked him to invite her again for a proper dinner and offered to make something special. This made him furious and he hit me; when I threatened to call the cops he said I would be the one to be deported, for I had no citizenship.

In August, I became pregnant. His family wanted a son when all I wanted was a healthy baby to bring blessing in my life. My pregnancy was normal and healthy but difficult because of the stress. Instead of maternity clothes I was given his sister's old clothes and was not allowed to eat what I craved.

In May, Allah blessed me with a healthy daughter, Zoya, the coolness of my eyes. H was happy to be a father, so happy that he forgot I was the mother. I was not allowed to shop for Zoya. Daily H came home and fixed her diaper, saying I was totally incompetent.

In December we moved to a new house.

2007

The less attention I paid to him the more things came out in the open. After returning from one of our US trips I found used contraceptives under my bed. When I told H not to give our house keys to his friend, I was beaten. When I told him his friends had offered to disclose his secrets to me if I agreed to have relations with them, H said I was overreacting. His friends tried to get fresh with me, touching me when I served them snacks during their visits while their wives discussed twosomes and threesomes during conversations. It was shocking to see this among these practicing Muslims and active volunteers at the community mosque.

2008

I tried to bear the abuse only for Zoya's sake. Having no family support and belonging to a community where a broken relationship was blamed on the woman, I had no option but to stay. I felt insecure in his circle and to keep my dignity I started wearing hijab and abayah. I lost all interest in dressing up and using fragrances.

At the end of 2008 I got pregnant again. I prayed for a son believing everything would get better after a boy.

2009

On January 9, our anniversary, while cleaning I found H's pseudonymous email account open with pornographic notifications and email exchanges with his friends about gay porn. I wanted to run away somewhere and not see his face. Since that day I stopped sharing the bed with H and started sleeping with Zoya.

I got my G1 and was allowed to drive because Zoya was starting school soon and H wanted to save carpooling expense.

In Pakistan my stepsister faced another failed marriage.

After one of my prenatal appointments, when H left for work, Zoya came to me and asked: "Ammi, are you going for an abortion?" The question puzzled me, since we had no satellite or cable at home for her to pick up this notion and I asked where she heard it. She said Daddy was talking to someone over the phone. I tried to distract her, saying there was no such word, but she protested, "No, it is a word because I asked Daddy and he said abortion is a way to clean germs in the stomach."

I had to admit the definition was pretty creative. I confronted H. I had kept quiet about the hickeys, the condoms in his office bag, his friends' wives' pictures in his cell phone, and he forcefully using me while watching porn. But now I had to draw the line for my children's sake. During our argument he pinned me against the wall, saying he could make me a vegetable and easily replace me.

In July I was blessed with a son, Haseeb, the strength of my heart. Zoya was the caring big sister since day one. Even at three and a half she knew how to help me during diaper change and calm Haseeb when he cried.

2010

H started taking Zoya out for drives to call on people he was involved with. Zoya started repeating his conversations. One day H got infuriated and started an argument using abusive language. I told him it was time for him to reap what he had sowed, and he pushed me down the stairs. He dragged me to our bedroom and banged my head against the wall. I called Pa to complain.

H called me a snake, sitting on the children's money that came from the government. He wanted to transfer it to his account but I was willing to transfer funds only into a joint account.

H's brother contacted Pa in Pakistan, claiming H was in a difficult marriage with a wife who was a misfit mother, who never cooked and failed to fulfill her duties of a wife.

Pa started planning his visit, telling me to be cautious and gather proof of my treatment and to either walk out safely with my children or use it in court. I started doing that, but I was not as smart as H.

H's friend openly started asking him for house keys so he could visit as often as he liked. Regardless, I consider myself blessed for no one raped me other than my husband.

2011

In September his family came from the US for a wedding and stayed at my house. H's sister accused me of acting pious while her henpecked brother served me like a slave. I was called ungrateful and advised to be a better wife or I would be sent back. I was replaceable and he deserved a better life. I was reminded that I came from a dysfunctional family where my sister had two failed marriages and my mother had abandoned me.

The night before Zoya started school, I was preparing her school uniform when H started yelling at me for not being ready. He called his sister and they both started yelling at me on a conference call. I was threatened to be thrown out without my children. I was grilled till four AM, and after a nap when I woke up to drop Zoya, H pushed me away, warning me to stay away from his children. He dropped

Zoya at school.

I called Pa, and H spoke to him, saying I was no longer wanted in his house and Pa should come to collect me soon. I tried to leave the room when H banged my head against the wall and threw me on the bed and I started bleeding after hitting the foot board.

H left for work and later that afternoon I dropped my bank card with a friend to keep it safe and asked my neighbour to scan the passports, for I had decided to leave with my children. I emailed everything to Pa and asked him to arrange three tickets. Pa asked me to be careful and call the police if I needed to. I knew that the police would arrest H for abuse, but I did not want to scar my children's lives with the memory of the police arresting H. More importantly I was afraid of losing my children, for H had said that the parent with a stable income got custody.

The next few days H brought food for me which made me sick, hence I started refusing food from elsewhere. One morning I wanted to drop Zoya to school but, he asked me to first eat what he had brought and when I resisted he said he would not kill me because I still had the children's money and he forcefully fed me something which looked like a biscuit and tasted weird.

I started feeling sick, suffocated, and breathless by the time we reached school. H told the women at school that I was sick and they advised him to take me to my doctor.

H took me home and said he was taking Haseeb to the park and his friend had the house keys to come over. I started crying, knowing what he meant and tried calling Pa, but H took the cordless from me. Before I could think or regain my senses I heard him saying over the phone, "She is crying uncontrollably and I have my two-year-old with me." He said he had called police to take me away. I threatened to tell everything to the police. He said if I wanted to be with my children and stay in this country I would have to stay quiet.

The police came and asked many questions. I recall saying, "He is a wonderful husband." They suggested I see a doctor. I went upstairs to get Haseeb's diaper bag while the police waited outside the house. I was packing the bag when H instructed me to remain quiet, and if I said anything I would regret that for the rest of my life. I agreed to stay quiet knowing I would soon leave with my children.

He dropped Haseeb at his friend's house and walked me to the hospital, where, while we waited, he told me he would leave once the doctor came and I would not see my children as I had failed as a wife.

I tried leaving the hospital but was taken to a separate room. All I remember was yelling that I was a citizen and they could not keep me without my consent. I gained my senses in the mental ward at the hospital. I asked to see Zoya and Haseeb and was told the doctor did not approve. I asked how I had ended up there, and H's cousins asked me to tell the doctors I had severe PMS and often had such episodes. I was discharged after ten days, to follow up with a psychiatrist.

H hacked my email account to delete everything I had saved as proof. He came to all my psychiatric appointments and I never felt safe enough to tell the doctor what actually had happened. In December H took me to the United States to send me to Pakistan after I had apologized to his family. I wanted to take Zoya and Haseeb with me but was told they were not replaceable.

At Karachi airport Pa could not recognize me.

2012

After two months, my in-laws contacted me for a reconciliation. I spoke to H, agreeing to give the money if he gave me Zoya and Haseeb, and he insulted me again. Pa's sisters were not in favour of a divorce, so after many discussions I decided to come back.

Zoya and Haseeb were excited to see me while H told everyone I was mentally sick. He kept coming regularly to my psychiatric appointments. Once he did not and I managed to share a few things with the psychiatrist, who suggested marriage counselling and called H to discuss the option. H assured him he would do whatever was necessary for my treatment. When I reached home, he hit me with a laptop and began to strangle me. The doctor did not bring up counselling again, and I became quiet.

Haseeb started picking up his father's language and rage, hitting me with anything that came to hand. I had accepted this as my life and H finally transferred the funds from my account into his.

2013

In February Pa was on his deathbed; the doctor had given up on him. Bhai asked me to visit and H sent me to Karachi for a few days. Within a few days Pa came out of coma and was able to sit on a chair. I told him I was very happy and things had changed completely for me. Pa called H to thank him for being a good son-in-law. He apologized for not telling me about my real mother, and I suggested we talk about that the next morning, when he came home. The next day Allah decided to make it easy for Pa and leave me unanswered. Three days later I returned to Canada.

H added life threats to his abuse, saying now I had nowhere to go. I told my psychiatrist I wanted to leave H. The psychiatrist asked me if I had plans to marry again, and after a few appointments he told H he should let me go. H refused, saying I had no one and would be a liability to my family.

H told me that now that he had the money he would kill me, and easily prove that I overdosed on my medication. I tried leaving him. After failing to book tickets online I found that my bank card was cancelled. I emailed Pa's younger brother, who was a travel agent in Dubai, for help. He asked for scans of all the passports and told me to reach the airport while he booked our flight. I found our hidden passports and saw that Zoya's passport was expired. I could not separate Zoya and Haseeb so I asked my uncle to arrange one ticket and kept all my educational documents in a small bag with basic essentials and a change of clothes.

I left home and called a lady doing carpool to pick Zoya up. I closed my bank account, which had some money. I called a cab and locked my car keys in the trunk.

I reached Karachi, where Bhai supported my decision while my aunts reminded me how Allah does not like a broken home. I called H to say I would file for divorce once I was back. In April I enrolled in a Montessori Diploma program. I called every day before school to talk to Zoya and Haseeb. After a few weeks H said the kids had better things to do and I managed to have one Skype session with Zoya, and Haseeb was not allowed to talk to me.

A few months later, H messaged me to check my email urgently. He had divorced me through email as per Sharia. He stopped taking my calls and messages. I called the Canadian Consulate in Islamabad to find out if my citizenship was still valid. They advised me to return to Toronto and get Legal Aid.

My passport had expired and I could not apply for a renewal since my citizenship card was in Canada. I tried to get legal aid in Canada, but very few lawyers replied; one lawyer agreed to take my case if I paid a thousand dollars as a retainer. I had no money and was turned down.

2014

H's family contacted my aunts and uncle, asking them not to let me travel to Canada, since that would disturb Zoya and Haseeb. His brother wanted my bank information, to transfer my mehr (the amount paid to a bride after the marriage contract), but I refused. My uncle asked me to keep him away from my problems.

I received my citizenship card and applied for a passport after a friend made the payment. A school friend contacted me on Facebook and insisted to pay for my ticket to Toronto and also arranged a place for me to stay. I met both Zoya and Haseeb at school, taking whatever gifts I could afford. They had been told Daddy had a new wife because Ammi was never coming back. After that H called Children's Aid (CAS) saying I had tried to abduct the children and in the past had tried to kill them as well.

CAS wanted my psychiatrist's approval and once it was received they arranged supervised access. This meant that the visits would be at my in-laws' or H's friend's place, where they tried to harass me more.

I was hired as a manager at a local restaurant to work on weekends and within months my supervisors tried to get fresh, with inappropriate touching and lewd remarks. I left.

January 2015

A week from my court date regarding my children, my lawyer informed me that there was postponment. I had seen my kids only twice since I returned, and I was behind in my rent payments. I asked for an emergency motion.

February 2015

By now I was eating once a day or fasting; extreme weather conditions and no winter boots turned my toes blue by the end of the day. On the day before the emergency motion my lawyer informed me that it had been cancelled. The next morning, I skipped school to visit the court and learned that my lawyer had not communicated with the court for the last three months. Everest College, which I was attending, was shut down by the ministry and I was with no education, no job, and broke with a $12000 OSAP loan. My legal aid certificate had expired, and my lawyer had no explanation. Now I had a scheduled case conference and no lawyer.

March 2015

After contacting numerous lawyers, I found one who took my case. When my psychiatrist's letter was provided in court, mentioning my nervous breakdown as a result of an abusive marriage, and stating that there were no mental concerns, H claimed that the psychiatrist had a close relationship with me and was biased. The judge ordered supervised access and property appraisal.

April 2015

The supervised access centre requires both parties to call and open a file in order to proceed. I have called three times in the last month, and they still haven't heard from H. A woman from a food bank delivers me food, and after almost six months I am able to eat at least two meals a day.

Dreams of Kabul

LAILA RE

I WAS BORN ON June 4, 1987 in Kabul. My mother happily named me Laila. She loved the name for three reasons: it means "night" in Arabic, and is often used to describe holy nights; it refers to the classical Persian love story, "Layla & Majnun"; and it is the first part of the Shahada, the Islamic creed. This is what she told me when I asked her what my name means. She was very proud of her choice; it was as though she had planted a beautiful story in me.

My mother passed away from a rare cancer called lung sarcoma on December 29, 2010. She was in palliative care during the last three days of her life. We watched her pass away painfully, one breath at a time. Her name was Messrie, her mother having named her after Egypt, which used to be called "Mesir." She didn't like how her name was pronounced in English because it sounded like the word "misery."

It is strange how in English it took on a meaning that was unfortunately so fitting to her life in late adulthood. Having escaped civil war with her family and left all she knew and loved forever behind, she was in misery. We were all in that emotional state due to our state of limbo. I always believed as a child that we would return to Afghanistan. Every year in Canada meant another year away from my roots. The more years passed since my arrival in Toronto in the winter of 1991, the more distant I felt, and this always scared me. I don't want to lose my mother tongue, Dari (Farsi). I try to preserve it so I can pass it on when I have my own children one day. I feel that it is the only thing left of my ancestors.

The story of my immigration to Canada began in 1989 when I was two, when my parents carried me across the Afghanistan-Pakistan border. I was the youngest of three daughters; my older sisters were five and eight. We travelled over the mountains by foot like all Afghan refugees escaping the civil war, which lasted from 1989 to 1992. In Islamabad, Pakistan, where we arrived, we lived as refugees before being sponsored to come to Canada.

My youngest sister—the fourth and last daughter—was born in Islamabad; my mom was actually in a car accident while pregnant with her. During our time in Pakistan, my mother started a women's newspaper and had a sewing business at home. She had earned a Bachelor of Journalism at Kabul University. It was in Kabul where she met my father, at her newspaper workplace when she was a reporter. My parents wanted us to have the same opportunities they had while growing up, which in Pakistan would not have been possible as Afghan refugees. This was why we moved to Canada.

They sacrificed their lives for our futures, moving to a country with a dominant language, culture, and religion that were completely different to theirs; they became nobodies and had to start from nothing. Neither of them spoke English fluently. It was a risk raising their children in an alien place, but they put their trust in it. Canada seemed progressive and promising. They let public schooling take over much of our upbringing, which was the source of much of our later identity crises, family breakdown, and cultural discontinuity.

My parents had to struggle financially. They worked at low-paying jobs with degrading treatment. They had four young girls depending on them and had to deal with a welfare system aggressively pushing them to become independent. We lived in a shelter for a few months when we first arrived in Toronto, but thanks to my father's persistence, we managed to get a public housing apartment.

Since my parents were stressed, busy and unable to understand English well, they could not be fully involved in our education. But they would remind us to study and focus on schooling. None of my sisters or I wore hijabs ("chadors" in Farsi). We didn't get a chance to learn to read or write in Farsi. We also didn't get a chance to attend Islamic classes. We didn't have many relatives so we also barely celebrated Muslim holidays. My identity as an Afghan and a Muslim was invisible in public and to myself.

Until grade four, we lived in the east end of Toronto. It was an ethnically, linguistically, and culturally diverse neighbourhood. I loved it and felt at home with my neighbours and classmates. The building we lived in, however, wasn't safe for us four little girls due to maintenance problems and security. My father often complained to Community Housing and recorded every undue incident. After we all got trapped in the elevator once, we were transferred to a new home. We moved to the west end, where I spent the rest of my childhood and teenage years. Our house was in a mixed-income neighbourhood; most of the homes were private and the residents were of European-Jewish descent. I never fitted in and I was depressed there. Both of my closest friends were Muslims, one a Somali and the other a Jamaican. We all lived on the same block.

My family and I would shop at the local flea market and the local mall. Summer times were spent watching TV and playing at the park or the swimming pool. Except for my fourth and fifth grade teachers, I hated everything else at school and didn't learn much. I made my first and only Afghan friend in high school, but she was more an acquaintance. I never had an Afghan or Muslim community to belong to either. I learned and preserved everything I could about my roots through the casual interactions with my parents. As long as we did not drink or do drugs, stay out late or overnight, or have boyfriends, they were content. They would remind us to try to speak Farsi at home, since our Farsi was becoming poorer. My mother would also encourage us to pray with her once in a while.

There was less and less hope of returning to Afghanistan. The Taliban regime took over much of the country in the early 1990s and installed a repressive government that imposed the harshest conditions for both men and women. There were reports of women losing their rights and men forced to follow extremist practices. Art, music, and partying were banned. No TVs. No cameras. No Internet. Not even kite-flying.

During the 1990s, I was concerned about my country and its people. My life at school was detached from my personal life; I did not trust and became disengaged from that Eurocentric institution, especially because rarely was there any discussion of the causes of many of the local and global issues. At that time, I got my political education through hip-hop artists, particularly Tupac "2pac" Amaru Shakur. I lived to just kill time. This emotional instability and confusion was a major distraction and impediment to my growth and relationships.

I was in grade 10 when 9/11 occurred. I was in gym class when the teacher stopped our activity and took us to the cafeteria to watch CNN. I saw the first tower burning, and I sat there and watched with surprise as the second tower was hit. I remember some girls crying. I was shaking inside because I knew that this event had to be Afghanistan-related. Ahmad Shah Massoud—commander of the Northern Alliance—was in talks with Europe to help him defend Afghanistan from the Taliban and Al-Qaeda. He warned the world that what was going on in Afghanistan would directly impact the West. He was assassinated two days before 9/11 by a suicide bomber.

The school was evacuated and everyone was standing outside, but I had no one to talk to about my thoughts. I was just worried for my country. I believed that whatever attention or help Afghanistan received would not be in its interests and long-term peace. When the Taliban regime was taken out by the US-led NATO military campaign, my parents were hopeful and happy for Afghanistan's future. My mother visited Afghanistan in 2007 and 2012. She was actually robbed at gunpoint during her travel from Kabul to Panjsher, her family village. Panjsher is also where Ahmad Shah Massoud was born and where he is buried.

There was a surge of discrimination towards Muslims post-9/11, though I personally didn't experience any Islamophobic or racist attacks. Most of my close friends were people of colour who were aware of racism. I did hear racist "jokes" about Afghans, but they weren't directed at me. I saw such comments as ignorant and their perpetrators as victims of brainwashing. I knew that Afghans desired peace but the world never helped us when we endured years of the Taliban regime. The mainstream news media and popular culture perpetuated stereotypes of Muslims and Afghans, and this just made me more distrustful and critical of the society and culture I lived in.

Once I graduated from high school, I was planning to find a job, but I realized then that I wanted to become a teacher, which required being accepted by a university. I did not have the grades for that. So I returned to high school to improve my grades, which I successfully did at a different high school. After that I became quite the academic "nerd" for the next few years. I was accepted at York University where I earned three degrees: Bachelor of Arts, Bachelor of Education and Master of Education. The last one came with a full scholarship and a Teaching Assistant position in my second year.

I learned much about the world around me in terms of its economic, political, and cultural systems. I did peace activism on campus for Palestine, First Nations, DR Congo, and Afghanistan. I felt intellectually empowered, and understood better that Afghanistan, like many other nations, was a proxy state for imperialism. My birthplace was a region that had been used by two superpowers—the United States and the Soviet Union—during their cold war. The current instability in Afghanistan is due to continuous foreign presence in order to maintain their strategic interests.

It was when I was in graduate school that my mother's sarcoma returned and worsened. Emotionally, I was becoming a wreck but I kept calm. When I was finally near finishing my education, my mother was close to dying. The sarcoma led to the amputation of her left leg, and she was unable to work and remained at home for the first time since coming to Canada. Until then I never had the time during which to enjoy living and bonding with my mother. Now I finally got to see my mother more often at home and know her better.

I was either at home, school, or work. My hobby was community activism or organizing. After my mother passed away, an identity crisis hit me. I was in my final semester of school and transitioning into the real world. I had no idea who to be and who to please. My father was retired. My sisters had their own lives that seemed to be more thriving than mine, except for my second sister who had been in a group home since she was thirteen. She was twenty-six now and still recovering. I was twenty-four years old with a strong academic foundation but a shaky emotional inner life. I was grieving my mother, dealing with built-up fears and having little faith in anything. I rebuilt myself by focusing on myself solely, after I suddenly moved out from my father's home. My personal development and inner peace were my main focus.

Now at twenty-seven and having lived on my own as an Afghan Muslim woman for three years, I can say that I have grown through my experiences. I self-published a book of 117 chronological poems set between April 2013 and July 2014, which deal with my experience of living on my own for the first time. I haven't visited Afghanistan yet.

It is sad that I will not see our native land with them, as I always dreamed of doing as a little girl. I do hope that I will be able to visit it in my lifetime. I know I will cry all the tears I shed from the time I was a three-year-old girl to when I became an adult woman whose feet finally found their way home. Insha'Allah (God Willing).

This poem from my book of poetry "Pieces to Peace" is titled

"Where did you cry?" and it is dedicated to the memory of my
mother.

where did you cry mommy
when your home was no longer a home?

did you cry on the train?
or when you stepped right out of the door?
or did you hold it in?
waiting to find a sanctuary you can call yours?
did you want to come back,
back to your family?
or did you dread it?
and just did what had to be done,
playing the maternal role,
to be the rock of the family
but where did you cry
when it couldn't be held in any more?

i want to know . . .

with all the pain
you bore
all the loss
you faced
where did you cry?

i really want to know . . .

i want to cry with you
when you sat alone to travel here and there all day away from us
i want to cry with you
when you waited to receive little pay for all your dignity
   sacrificed
i want to cry with you
when you sat silently at home

while your body was there but your mind unaware
i want to cry with you
when you felt stuck
in your past
in your circumstance

i wish i was there to cry with you
in those moments that you wished you could leave
and walk away . . .

who did you confide in,
who knew your suffering?

i know you cried
daily on the inside
but where did you cry,
when the tears could no longer hide?

i wish i was there,
to cry with you . . .
because i cried on the inside too,
a daughter, at home, just missing you
wondering why i never saw my mother's face
all day, all night long . . .

The Story of My Life

DUAA AL-AGHAR

I GREW UP IN IRAQ in a very nice family which consisted of my mom, my dad, one sister, and two brothers. We lived in peace until 1979, when Saddam Hussein took away my uncle and my dad because they were Shia religious leaders. After one month they released my dad, but he was depressed and he was also crying a lot. I asked him why he was crying, and he told me that he lost his brother. He didn't tell me the whole story because I was only five years old, but I found out later that Saddam's people had dissolved my uncle in acid right in front of my dad.

Two months later they surrounded my home and my dad tried to hide but no luck. The police kicked the door open and entered the house and took my dad away. I saw his hands being tied together with chains, and then I never saw him again.

We heard that Saddam hanged my dad. Many years after that tragedy, I decided I would be a strong woman so I could face challenges without fear. I finished studying computer engineering and then got a master's degree but because I was the daughter of the enemy of Saddam, I did not have a lot of opportunities in Iraq.

In the second year of university I met my lovely husband, and after I finished my master's degree I got married. After six months we decided to leave Iraq and seek opportunities outside my country.

Therefore we went to Libya and thank God we found jobs in the countryside for the first three years and then we moved to a city called Misrataa. It was a beautiful city. We worked in a well-known institute as professors of computer engineering. We had a lovely life in Libya, but after five years of moving to Misrataa, my husband decided to continue his education in Canada. So we applied as skilled workers and came to Canada as immigrants.

We landed in Canada on May 11, 2006. It was raining that day. I liked the airport as everything was so organized and neat. Our friend from Kitchener came to pick us up. We also chose to live in Kitchener.

The first thing we did was improve our English skills by attending an ESL school. I stayed in the school only ten months and then joined the New Canadian program. They advised us to start as volunteers, so I started teaching computers as a volunteer at the Salvation Army and fixing computers at KW Access Ability in Waterloo. After only a few weeks of working as a volunteer with KW Access Ability they offered me a job. It was a one-year contract as a project manager which they renewed for two more years.

After my contract finally ended I started looking for another job and after one month I found a job at the Islamic Humanitarian Services where I work today. I love this job; the staff are friendly and my manager is kind and compassionate. Here I also joined different groups such as Abrahamic Peace Builder, Interfaith Grand River, and a women's group talking about faith and religious accommodation.

Education is very important for everyone especially women. I believe that knowledge is more important than wealth because money cannot buy knowledge, whereas knowledge can help to make wealth. I spent more than fifteen years studying and getting my master's degree in computer engineering. I plan to finish my PhD study as soon as my husband finishes his.

We have been married for almost eighteen years and have two kids, a son, Ali, and daughter, Aethar, who were both born in

Libya. I am a religious, practicing Muslim. I say my five prayers every day, fast in the month of Ramadan, recite Quran, and supplicate regularly. I don't want to say more about my practice because it will be riya (riya in any of its forms amounts to shirk, "verily, one who works for the people, his reward lies with them, and one who works for God his reward lies with God."). I don't drink or smoke.

I am grateful to be Muslim. Islam unites Muslims because we all have one deen (religion), one God, Allah almighty, one prophet, Muhammad (s.a.w.), and one qiblah that we all face in prayer. Islam is the rope of Allah which He ordered us to hold fast by saying in surat Al-Emran, (verse 103 and 105),

> And hold fast, all of you together, to the rope of Allah (i.e. this Quran), and do not divide among yourselves. And remember Allah's favour on you, for you were enemies and He joined your hearts together, so that by His Grace, you became brethren (in Islamic Faith), and you were on the brink of a Pit of Fire, and He saved you from it. Thus Allah makes His Ayat (proofs) clear to you, that you may be guided.

Then He said,

> And be not as those who divided and differed among themselves after the clear proofs had come to them. It is they for whom there is an awful torment.

I thank Allah who gave me such a wonderful husband who supports me in everything I do, who lifts me up when I am down, who understand me like none other, who helped me achieve my dreams and who believes in me no matter what.

The Quran indicates that men and women are spiritual equals. The Quran 4:124 states:

> If any do deeds of righteousness be they male or female and have faith, they will enter Heaven, and not the least injustice will be done to them.

I started wearing my beautiful hijab when I was in grade three. Nobody forced me to wear it. I like wearing hijab because I feel protected. When women wear hijab nobody looks at them with sexual desire, they will look at their minds and intellect. A woman wearing hijab is a visible sign of Islam. While Muslim men can blend easily into any society, Muslim women are often put on the line, and forced to defend not only their decision to cover their heads but also their religion.

Islam prohibits all forms of oppression and injustice (Quran 5:8; 41: 135; 42:42-43). Muslim scholars agree that Islam does not allow any form of abuse. It is narrated that the Prophet Muhammad (pbuh) said, "The most perfect of believers in belief is the best of them in character. The best of you are those who are the best to their women." And also, "The best among you are those who are kindest to their wives."

Like the Stones of a Mosaic

JENNA M EVANS

I COME FROM A FAMILY that can be best described as a mosaic of different religions, races, and cultures. My mother, Insaf, whose name means "justice", was born and raised in Somalia, but she has a diverse background with Indian, Somali, Yemeni, and Afghani heritage. She speaks Somali, Urdu, Arabic, and English, and is a chameleon, capable of integrating seamlessly with multiple cultural groups. My father is of Welsh origin and converted to Islam when he married my mother in a small ceremony in Riyadh, Saudi Arabia, where they were both working at the time. I came along shortly after.

My parents' marriage ended amicably in England five years later, primarily because my father no longer practiced Islam. My mom and I moved to Jacksonville, Florida, which is where she met and married my step-father, a Somali PhD student at the University of Florida. I soon began calling him "dad" and as we moved west, to Texas and then to California, and as our family grew bigger, the distance between my biological father and I grew wider. Twelve years would pass before we would meet again, and twenty years before I would be reunited with my Welsh grandparents.

My mother has been an Islamic Studies and Quran teacher for as long as I can remember. I learned how to practice Islam from her as well as from attending Sunday school throughout my childhood. I even worked as a Sunday school teacher as a teenager for six months. In this role, I integrated Islamic studies and English language curricula to create a literacy program for Muslim children. I earned the Girl Scout Gold Award, the highest award in Scouting, as a result. I was very active in the Muslim community, leading weekly sessions for children, participating in youth groups, attending courses, speaking at events, and volunteering with the Muslim Students' Association at both my high school and university campuses. In 2003, at the age of 17, I made the decision to wear the Islamic head covering, the hijab. One year later, I got married.

When the average person hears about an eighteen-year-old Muslim girl getting married, they likely think "how sad" and "it must have been arranged." I was well-aware at the time of what many of our non-Muslim family friends were thinking. They saw me as a hard-working young woman with promise. I was in my second year of university with an accomplished resume of academic achievements and work experience. My goal was to go to medical school.

My husband, Habib, and I were introduced to one another through our families. My grandmother, Badrunissa (meaning "full moon of the women"), knew my husband's parents, who are originally from Pakistan, when they were in their twenties. They lost touch over the years and just happened to reconnect in 2003, almost forty years later. My grandmother immediately wanted to set me up with her long-lost friend's son, and soon talked our mothers into facilitating an introduction. The only catch was we lived in California and he lived in Ontario, Canada. My husband and I were aware of the fact that our families had hopes we would "hit it off", which made for several very awkward conversations via email and telephone. However, a friendship blossomed between us and he proposed within a few months.

Given that my own biological parents were divorced, I was nervous and indecisive. I changed my mind frequently, even retracting my eventual "yes" to contemplate more. I prayed fervently during this time, asking for God's guidance. Although I was young, I was well-aware that love was not enough to sustain a marriage. I was searching primarily for compatibility in lifestyle and values. Although Habib and I are complete opposites in many ways and have had our fair share of domestic disputes, we have always been on the same page when it comes to the things that count—and we now have more than twelve years worth of stories and photos to prove it.

I fervently disagree with "forced marriages." Unfortunately, this is still widely practiced among Muslims, though it has no basis in Islam. But not all arranged marriages are forced marriages. My marriage was "arranged" in the sense that our families introduced us and strongly encouraged us, but the ultimate decision was ours.

I have no regrets about marrying young. Today, we encourage youth to spend their twenties "finding themselves" and building a career; marriage is strongly discouraged. I was able to explore my interests, complete my education, build my career, give back to my community, and travel *while* nurturing my marriage. Marriage did not slow me down, it honed my maturity and cultivated my independence. It brought me to Canada, a country I am proud to call home. While married, I taught English as a Second Language full-time for one year at the Regina Huda School, an Islamic school in Saskatchewan. As a Girl Guide, I helped launch the Girls for Safer Communities program, represented Canada at the Women Deliver Conference in Malaysia in 2013, and currently lead a local Ranger unit for high school girls. I also volunteered and worked as a freelance writer. I earned a Bachelor's Degree in Health Management from York University and in 2013, at the age of 28, I completed a PhD in Health Services Research from the University of Toronto. In addition to my own ambition and work ethic, I attribute my success to my husband's unwavering support and to my faith, which kept me away from time-consuming distractions.

Like most youth, however, I did experience an identity crisis in my late teens and early twenties. As a Muslim woman wearing the hijab, I had a strong desire for a Muslim name that reflected how

I felt on the inside and how I looked on the outside. I wanted to change my name from "Jenna Evans" to "Jannah Zakaria," which involved taking my husband's last name. However, in Islam women are not required or encouraged to take their husband's last name. My husband suggested that I wait and consider whether or not I wanted to take this step. Over time, I realized that my name made me no more or no less a Muslim; and it was my most concrete link to my Welsh roots.

My identity issues resurfaced a few years later. It was seven years since I began wearing the hijab. I was one of only a handful of women who wore the hijab in Regina, Saskatchewan. People often stared at me. My response was to grab my husband's hand lovingly and give them a huge smile—my way of saying "I am just like you." I wore the hijab with pride and welcomed the opportunity to act as an ambassador for my religion and way of life. However, even though I had never experienced prejudice or discrimination first-hand, by 2009 my feelings towards the hijab had begun to change and in early 2010, after months of deliberation, I made the difficult decision to stop wearing it.

It is hard to describe my emotions at the time. I no longer wanted to be easily identifiable as a Muslim and I began to view the hijab as a burden. The role as "ambassador" that I had embraced for years now felt heavy on my shoulders. I felt a strong desire to keep my religious beliefs and practice to myself. Watching the news on a daily basis (my husband and many of my friends are news junkies) meant constant exposure to what radical Muslims were doing in the name of Islam. I was also preparing for a visit to Lancaster, England, my childhood home, where my father and grandparents lived. Twenty years had passed since I left Lancaster. Although I met my father briefly twice in London, this would be the first time we would spend more than just a few hours together. I was excited and nervous. I did not know what to expect. The fact that they lived in a small town in northern England, not in a large city with more diversity, added to my fears. I wanted more than anything to be able to integrate with them, to feel like "family." I saw the hijab as a potential barrier. The combination of feelings I was already experiencing and my looming family reunion created a tipping point and led to my decision to take off the hijab. I made a promise to myself, however, that even without the hijab I would continue to dress modestly. That is a promise I have kept to this day.

Do I regret removing the hijab? A small part of me does. I wish that I had been more confident and stronger in my faith. I have friends in the US and in Canada who have experienced discrimination first-hand as a result of their hijab or pressure from their families to remove their hijab, yet they did not do so. So why did I? Removing my hijab is not something I am proud of, but I was ultimately content with my decision and have had no intention since then of putting it back on—but that does not mean I never will. I am fortunate to come from a family and to live in a country where I have the freedom to make that choice for myself.

It has been six years now since I removed my hijab, but I put it on when I pray, read Quran, or visit a mosque. My husband and I attend a mosque near our home; we chose it because our views and values seemed to align well with those of the attending community, because of the programs and activities offered, and because the imam's voice when he recites the Quran is so beautiful. In 2013, our mosque hosted a multi-faith women's event called "Women Gathering," which included singing by a church choir and a speech by a female Buddhist monk, among other speakers and activities. I respect the mosque administration for supporting multi-faith dialogue and collaboration through events such as this. At our previous mosque I felt unhappy and unwelcome. The women were made to enter through a side door and given a tiny room with no view of the imam, which sometimes made it difficult to follow along during prayer. I once went to pray right after school, wearing a trench coat, hijab, and long shirt over my jeans; my outfit was considered inappropriate and an elderly woman at the door scowled at me and handed me a skirt to wear over my clothing. I was surprised and hurt by her abrupt behaviour. Our places of worship must not become places of judgment. Our mosques must be havens that attract and welcome all Muslims.

On the same note, I disapprove of mosques that cater to specific ethnic and cultural groups. Programs can be tailored to the needs of specific subgroups of Muslims, but segregating them into different mosques based on demographic factors such as race, ethnicity, or gender is a step backwards. Muslims have long aspired to the ideal of *one ummah* (a united community), a vision that cannot be achieved if we continue to segregate.

I feel fortunate to live in Canada, where diversity and tolerance are strongly espoused values. The climate towards Muslims here is more positive than in many other places, including the United States, the United Kingdom, and Europe. But I fear that this could change at a moment's notice should terrorists succeed in committing violent acts in Canada. Every time I hear the words "bomb" or "mass murder" on the news, regardless of the location, I silently repeat "please don't be a Muslim" over and over in my head. I fight back tears when I hear of terrorist attacks led by Muslims, not only out of grief for the victims, but also out of shame and anger that the perpetrators commit these acts in the name of my religion. I sometimes make a conscious choice to avoid watching or reading the news. There are also frequent examples of blatant media hypocrisy in how events are presented or simply ignored.

My relationship with my non-Muslim grandparents and father has blossomed since my visit to Lancaster in 2010. I made two more trips to see them, and my father has come to visit me twice as well. My grandparents still remember and often use the word "Insha'Allah" (God-willing), which they grew accustomed to hearing my mom say when my parents were married. My father still knows how to recite Surah Fatiha (the opening chapter of the Quran). Between us there is a mutual appreciation and respect for each other's religion and choices.

Given my diverse background and experiences, I do contemplate how I will raise my future children. Having a family has always been a key goal of mine. However, my husband and I had agreed before marriage that my education would be our first priority. At the time, we could not have imagined that I would pursue a PhD! Because of that, we further delayed starting a family. By the time we started trying, we had been married for nine years. Unfortunately, we struggled to conceive. Minor fertility interventions failed and two and a half years passed.

During this difficult time, Islam was both a source of comfort and pain. My mom would constantly remind me, *inallahu ma'a sabireen* ("God is with those who are patient"). Islam teaches us that God knows what is best for us, that He never gives us a burden we cannot handle, that He tests us in different ways, and that our sins are expiated when we experience hardships. But it also says heaven is "under the feet of our mothers." The Prophet (peace be upon him) is quoted as saying "Do good to and serve your mother, then your mother, then your mother, then your father." I could not help wondering if I was less of a woman because I was not a mother. Negative and cynical feelings festered in me. Then I came across a Facebook post on infertility by the Islamic scholar, Omar Suleiman. It brought me to tears. It reminded me that two of the greatest women in Islam, Aisha bint Abu Bakr and Assiya bint Muzahim, never had children. Exactly one month after reading that article and without any medical intervention, I found out I was pregnant.

Now, as I prepare for my daughter's arrival, I am taken back to a family portrait we took in the summer of 2013. In that portrait, which shows my diverse extended family, I see the source of my child's most valuable education. My little one will grow up knowing that families are bound by shared experiences and emotions, not by blood, features, or skin tone. She will embody the essence of inter-racial, inter-cultural, and inter-faith diversity and acceptance. And I can only hope that she will live in a world where there are no contradictions between being a good Muslim and being a proud Canadian.

Finding God, Finding Me

CARMEN TAHA JARRAH

YOU'LL LIKELY WALK past me and not know that I am a daughter of the ancient Levant, that I trace my roots to the Phoenicians. You'll likely walk past me without knowing my religious beliefs. I am a Muslim. My hijab-free head is my protection from potential assault. I am not a walking stereotype or target, and prefer it that way these days. I am neither Sunni nor Shia. Although my parents call themselves Sunnis, I do not subscribe to any sect. I am a nameless hybrid, part Jewish, part Christian, part Muslim.

We are all shaped by our environment. I lived most of my life straddling two separate worlds, comfortable with both eastern and western cultures and languages, yet not quiet fitting into either, too white for one, not white enough for the other, stereotyped by both. In my youth, I sat silently on the fringes, too stupid about my ethnicity and religion to counter myths and stereotypes. I saw myself largely through western eyes. It took travels to the Middle East and beyond in search of the Arab and Muslim footprint, and decades of reading to undo the influence of pop culture and counter the propaganda, and reclaim my religion and culture, my identity.

It's not easy being a Muslim anywhere these days. A new word was created in the English lexicon, Islamophobia. In my life time, Islam has morphed from relative obscurity to an evil actor on the global stage, peered at and pontificated upon by self-proclaimed experts, politicians, and media pundits. Burqa, hijab, and niqab have become household terms. I went from feeling like I belonged in multicultural Canada to having fears of banishment.

I wonder how other Muslims, in particular the youth, are coping with the escalating phobia against Muslims—anti-Muslim demonstrations, laws banning Sharia, laws banning hijabs, growing opposition to building mosques, Muslim cemeteries and hijab-wearing soccer players, public burning of the Quran; there is even the occasional call for extermination. We are in a state of mass hysteria, suspended sanity. What is the solution?

"Read" was God's first commandment to Prophet Muhammad. This timeless message is ever more paramount today. It has been my life motto, a passion I instilled in my children. I humbly submit that some Muslims have forgotten God's first commandment. Reading, seeking knowledge, ensures that you emerge afterwards into the brilliant butterfly you were meant to be.

This is an abridged version of my story, an ordinary Muslim woman's path toward seeking knowledge and self-awareness, finding the "peace" in Islam.

Canada has been my home since November 18, 1958, long before Muslims entered the spotlight. It was a frigid day when I arrived in Edmonton with my Lebanese parents and three sisters from Brazil, where I was born. I was two. We settled in Lac La Biche, a small multiethnic Alberta town where my maternal grandparents lived and where a number of other Lebanese immigrants had settled. Our house sat on the outskirts of town, a small wood structure without indoor plumbing or central heating. My backyard, my world and classroom for ten years, was a fifteen-acre parcel of land, a mixed-wood forest of poplar, willow, and spruce, with a pond in the middle, a place to explore and experience Nature, the changing seasons. It is where I discovered God.

I spent winter months with my siblings building tunnels in the

snow and tobogganing. Spring was my favourite time, splashing
about in the rivulets during the snow melt, making necklaces and
anklets from yellow marsh flowers at the pond's edge, waiting for
the seeds in the garden to stir and poke through the black earth in
neat rows. Summer meant long days of freedom outdoors, forag-
ing for wild berries. Strawberries were the first to ripen followed
by raspberries, saskatoons and gooseberries, and later blueberries.
I made sling shots, built forts in the woods, climbed trees, played
"cowboys and Indians," and swam in the lake nearby. And there
were many opportunities for solitude. Filled with curiosity, I often
contemplated the flora and fauna around me, spent hours staring
in wonderment at the intricate pattern of a spider's web, a lair and
snare, watching ants carry twice their weight, wondering why bees
and butterflies visit flowers, why sheep bump and dogs hump.

I was fortunate to have learned early in my childhood to respect
Nature. This translated into humility toward God. I felt His majesty and mercy, a reverence without comprehension; the seeds
of my identity and religious beliefs, my interconnectedness with
others and Nature, were sown in my backyard.

My parents were illiterate immigrants with no money or trade,
struggling to eke out a living in a new land while learning its laws,
language, and traditions, trying to fit in while maintaining their
cultural and religious traditions. We dressed like the larger community; my mother did not wear a hijab and there was never any
talk about "having" to wear one. At the time, only elderly women
like my paternal grandmother wore a head cover, called a *mandeel*.
We ate Arabic food and socialized with relatives and the other Lebanese in town. My parents stopped speaking Portuguese, my first
language, and began conversing in Arabic at home. By the time I
started school, I had learned two languages but not one word of
English.

But I picked it up quickly; I did not appreciate being different
and simply wanted to fit in at school. I was also ashamed of being
poor; my lunch: peanut butter sandwiches made with paper-thin *saj*

bread, and I was teased for "eating paper." I remember wanting to be part of the Christmas scene, my "white" friends asking, "What did you get for Christmas?" Me lying, "I got an easy-bake oven." It was easier to lie than to explain my family did not celebrate Christmas, and besides they had no money for toys. But we were rich in other ways; and poverty was a great teacher.

My parents' belief in God was unshakeable; He was always on their lips. They abstained from pork and alcohol. We fasted during Ramadan, celebrated the two Eids, but my parents did not pray five times daily like they do now. I suspect survival left little time for prayer. Providing food, shelter, and clothing meant my father was away from home for months at a time, working on railroads and felling trees in the forests. Like many others in town, he also tried mink farming. Meanwhile, my mother had five more children. She too toiled: raising children, cooking, cleaning, growing her own food, pickling vegetables, canning fruit, baking bread.

Christianity also entered my world early, left an indelible imprint. Every morning, I stood with my classmates at Vera M Welsh Elementary School and recited the Lord's Prayer, then sang "O Canada" and "God Save the Queen." I did not give it much thought, it was what we did in school. My parents did not object. "There is only one God," my mother always said. And so it passed, I would recite the Lord's Prayer in the mornings and before I went to sleep, the fatiha.

I'd rather forget my teenage years. When I was thirteen, my family moved from my beloved Lac La Biche to Fort McMurray, a bigger town further north, before the oil sands boom. I lost my freedom overnight, became responsible for looking after my younger siblings while my parents worked as janitors in the evenings. They were strict—no going out, just to school and back. I was the only Arab in my school, and the only girl in eighth grade still waiting for puberty to kick in. After three years in Fort McMurray, I became gravely ill and needed care in the city. My father moved us to Edmonton, where I have lived since.

I married at nineteen, "before I opened my eyes," to quote an Arab proverb. It was not love at first sight or an arranged marriage. I was plain-looking, with a sticklike figure, and worried about becoming an old maid. And I was not brave enough to stray from traditions and wanted my parents' blessings. I did what was expected of a dutiful Arab daughter, maintained my chastity and married a Lebanese Muslim. I met my husband on the bus one autumn morning; handsome and with a worldly air, he told me I had beautiful eyes. Naïve and insecure about my looks, I fell in love with the idea of being in love, getting male attention for the first time. I loved school, wanted to attend university. And while my parents valued education, especially as illiterate immigrants, they gently steered me toward marriage. I suspected they prayed silently I would marry before, God forbid, I came home pregnant and brought shame to them.

I was blessed with two daughters and a son, all three of them precocious, and they became my life. I hunkered down, despite a dysfunctional marriage, as it turned out, doing double duty, juggling motherhood and full-time work. I strove to be the perfect mother, showered my children with love, surrounded them with books, helped them with homework, made nutritious meals, enrolled them in sports, took them to plays, took them on trips every year. I stressed the importance of learning. "School does not end after grade 12," I always told them. Thankfully, one became a doctor and two, lawyers.

Travelling to my ancestral homeland, Lebanon, for the first time was an eye-opener in many ways. Young and ill-informed, I went with pre-existing ideas about what it meant to be an Arab, influenced by Hollywood depictions, television programs, and the media: rich oil sheikhs, harems, belly dancers, deserts and camels. Camels? In Lebanon? I came across one, at the entrance of the ancient Roman temple in Baalbek, a tourist site. For a few liras I got to sit on the camel; after the camel rose to his feet, a photographer snapped my photo and the camel sat back down. It took travel and extensive reading to form a true picture of my Arabness and Muslimness.

More importantly, I remember how powerless I felt at not being able to read the signs in Arabic, as if I were deprived of one of my senses. For the first time I could relate to how my parents must have felt, and vowed to learn to read Arabic, learn the history of the Arabs and Muslim civilizations. I needed to be able to answer my children's questions about their identity, and to quench my own insatiable thirst for the truth.

Something else compelled me even more to learn to read Arabic. I was weary of being told that I could never get to the essence of the Quran, that is, Islam, through a translation. This made me even more determined. I had already acquired and read more than ten different English translations. While some Arabic words have no English equivalents, and while some verses in the Quran are metaphorical, some controversial and some lack unanimity in interpretation, and some are seemingly contradictory and admittedly beyond my nonscholarly grasp, still, the essence, the halal and haram were clear enough to me from the translations.

I refused to believe that an omniscient God would send a message in Arabic that excludes the majority of the 1.7 billion Muslims worldwide who speak a multitude of languages and would not be able to appreciate it without a translation. I refused to accept that God would limit the appreciation of the Quran by the majority and trust Islam to a select minority, mostly men. I refused to believe that God's message is too esoteric for me to learn, and to allow my religion to be dictated by an imam or scholar. The Quran tells us to confirm things for ourselves, that He is the ultimate teacher and helper.

So I began teaching myself classical Arabic by reading the Quran from cover to cover, over and over again. I made this part of my daily routine. My strategy involved listening to a recitation on CDs while following the written text. Gradually, I was able to recognize and read words without having to sound out each letter. I achieved three goals simultaneously, learning to read Arabic, increasing my vocabulary, and gaining a deeper appreciation of Islam. The Quran became an obsession. I'd get out of bed, warm up some milk, curl up on the couch with the Quran and read until my eyelids drooped. Call me delusional, but at times I sensed a presence, I'd like to believe it was God, helping me along.

I got into the habit of looking up key words, learned alternate meanings and different perspectives. I amassed a library of books, attended Quran classes at the mosque, memorized chapters, and learned the rules of *tartil* and *tajwid*. I read biographies of the Prophet, hadith literature, alleged sayings and actions of the Prophet compiled by Bukhari and Muslim, and learned that many of the *halals* and *harams* in Islam originate from hadith and have no basis in the Quran.

The years raced by, became a blur. In my late thirties, in between mothering and working, I began training in Tae Kwon Do, at the same gym where I had enrolled my son. Eventually we each earned a black belt, a big feat for someone like me who began with little flexibility and coordination. I won two gold medals in sparring at the provincial championships.

Then 9/11 happened.

And if it could get worse, one of the alleged hijackers turned out to be my husband's distant cousin. My surname cited in newspapers, television, and the Internet, I stayed home for two days, unable to face my coworkers. I was questioned by the RCMP after a "tip" from, I suspect, a fellow employee; threats were left on my phone; racist graffiti was scrawled on my husband's car. For the first time in Canada, I feared for my family's safety. To cope, I volunteered, participated in interfaith activities, and joined a local women's peace coalition. I continued reading; and by now the shelves in bookstores were filled with books: *The Trouble with Islam*, *What Is Right About Islam*, *The Other Islam*.

Here I was approaching fifty, dealing with the empty-nest syndrome, a failed thirty-two-year marriage, aging parents, and approaching retirement, asking, "Beyond being a daughter and wife, beyond motherhood, who is Karima? What is God's plan for me? What have I become. What do I want to become. What could I become?"

I always wanted to go back to school, thought that the dream would have to wait until after retirement. But I managed to get permission from my boss to attend classes during the day as needed. I earned a Bachelors in professional communications, graduating "with distinction," a goal that would bring me closer to fulfilling a childhood dream of writing my own book.

I also set aside time to satisfy another passion, travelling. It became my ultimate teacher. Not only did I experience diverse landscapes and cultures, I discovered something about myself after every journey, and felt blessed. I slept under the stars in the Serengeti and the Sahara. Swam in thermal hot springs in Turkey and floated over parts of Cappadocia in a hot air balloon at sunrise. I snorkelled off the coast of Zanzibar, and went cruising on the Nile, body surfing and white water rafting on the Ganges, parasailing in Vietnam, zip-lining in Zambia, trekking up mountainous jungles to glimpse gorillas in Uganda. I rode elephants in Cambodia and Zimbabwe, walked with lion cubs and rubbed one's belly and felt its heart beat beneath my fingertips. I observed hundreds of wildlife in their natural environment: a cheetah and her four cubs stalking a gazelle, leopards snoozing in the trees, an elephant herd at a watering hole, wildebeest as far as I could see. It felt as if I had beheld the face of God.

One journey in particular changed my destiny; this part of my story is still being written. As a member of the Arab Jewish Women's Peace Coalition, I travelled to the Holy Land in 2009 and went back the following two autumns. In 2010, to show my solidarity with displaced and dispossessed Palestinians, I volunteered to help them during the olive harvest. I returned as a "pilgrim" in 2011 with an interfaith group from Canada. I could not unhear or unsee the oppression I witnessed. I was dogged by a line of graffiti on

Israel's separation wall, "Now that I have seen, I am responsible."

I was driven to raise awareness about Israel's occupation by writing about my experiences, highlighting the stories of an oppressed people, stories of peace-builders, Israelis and Palestinians, stories rarely reported by western corporate media. It took me four years to complete a manuscript.

I have given you a glimpse into my story, my journey of self-learning. To conclude, I would like to leave you, my dear reader, with snippets of my beliefs concerning Islam. In my search for the many truths, what I thought was Islam sometimes was not. Issues I thought to be black and white turned out to be various shades of grey. The light-bulb moments I experienced felt like I had pulled a stray thread from a favourite sweater and watched it unravel before my eyes. In my lifetime I noticed Wahhabism permeate and twist Islam beyond recognition.

I'm an angry, disappointed Muslim with a number of pet peeves: the mixing of religion and politics, culture, and male egos; the confusion of the Quran with hadith, which were compiled centuries after the Prophet's death. I believe that many Muslims in Canada are followers mainly of hadith and don't know it. Imams and scholars place too much emphasis on dubious hadith and too little on Quran. What the Quran gave women with one hand the hadith took back with the other. While some hadith are consistent with the Quran and favourable to women, many hadith presented as sacred and on par with the Quran are racist and misogynistic, and contrary to Islam.

I do not believe for a moment that the Prophet was a misogynist; that he said a nation led by a woman will never succeed; or that he visited the gates of hell and observed that most of its inhabitants were women, not owing to some grievous sin, but because they were "ungrateful to their husbands"; or that three things interrupt a man's prayer: "dog, ass, and woman"; or that, "Had I ordered anyone to prostrate before anyone, I would have ordered women to prostrate before their husbands."

As for the controversial hijab, a tradition that predates Islam, in some countries wearing it is a crime, in others not wearing it is a crime. I believe in modesty, but many Muslims are too preoccupied with the female body and female behaviour, reducing the essence of Islam to a piece of cloth, and making women solely responsible for men's gazes and sexual urges. For some, the hijab symbolizes my degree of purity and religiosity, for others, my submission, oppression, and ignorance. I believe in having the choice to cover or uncover. Hijab is not definitive and mandatory.

Muslims need to read for themselves. We cannot continue following blindly, have our faith dictated by imams, religious scholars, or fundamentalists, our culture coloured by corporate media, political pundits, and Hollywood. We must lift back the veil of ignorance, nourish our souls with the dew of knowledge and heed God's first commandment to the Prophet. Reading is the one thing we can all do to grow and to remedy what ails our planet.

The Muslimah Who Fell to Earth

MUNIRAH MACLEAN

THIS STORY BEGINS at Mirabel Airport, a lofty, light-filled white albatross of a place in the middle of snowy, white fields not too far from Montreal.

I arrive. I get to Customs; I'm a small white British girl wearing a grey duffle coat with a Turkish kerchief on her head. My passport is stamped full: Europe, Turkey, Cyprus, India, Syria, Greece, and Bulgaria but (oops) I don't have a visa for Canada. I didn't have enough time on my last visit to England to get one. So I make duas. I learned the fatiha and several of the short surahs from the wife of Sheikh Nazim, Hajja Amina Hatun (May Allah sanctify her). I have been a Muslim for six months, I took Shahada and a pledge of allegiance to my sheikh of the Naqshbandi tariquat and got married all on the same day. I don't have a marriage certificate because I had a Turkish Sufi wedding in a mosque in Nicosia, Cyprus which wasn't even recognized as a state at that time.

"Hmm," says the official. "Bonjour," I say with a bright smile, then more duas and fatihas under my breath. I have come in on a one-way ticket. Naively, I tell him the truth. My Canadian-born husband of three months is on the other side of the gate waiting for me. The official sighs. "I'm not going to stamp your passport, you have to go to the British Consulate downtown right away."

Alhumdulillah! Thank you Allah! I have never heard of anyone getting through international customs without a passport stamp before or since.

I'm through! Welcome to Canada! Big Sky! Ibrahim is gorgeous! He is wearing a big fur hat and has a bushy Naqshbandi beard and warm brown eyes. He looks like a teddy bear. And on the subject of bears . . . yes, there is snow but I don't see any polar bears out of the car window on the drive to Parc Extension. I meet Davy, my new father-in-law who has come along to collect his son's newest bride. His car has a hole in the floor, but I don't find that unusual because in Margaret Thatcher's Britain, where I have come from, you are rich if you have a car at all. "All the other Jews have Cadillacs," he tells me earnestly, "but I was just a cutter so I worked for the money." Davy is gentle and humble but confused about his eldest son, who went to Jerusalem and returned a Sufi. After we arrive at the family duplex I meet Sylvia, my mother-in-law. She is wearing a coral pink velvet jogging suit and has come home from her second job. She doesn't like to sit still, she thinks it's lazy. She is, I realize, a clever woman with strong opinions about almost everything. She confides, "I liked the first one, her father had a shopping mall, the second one was a Quebecker, she only liked her own people." She is reserving judgment on me, the third wife in five years, the new one. I keep my thoughts to myself. With Allah's grace a miracle takes place, we become friends and my husband's family becomes my Canadian family for which I am forever grateful. Disparate elements, different worlds, but through the wisdom of the heart we come together. SubhanAllah (God is Glorious).

As a new wife, I knew that statistics were not on the side of a long-term marriage, but I decided this one was going to be different. I also knew about the reality of polygamy, having encountered two rather strange German-born women who were travelling together and were married to the same man. They were both recent converts to Islam, and had lived in a vegan commune previously. "Oh it's fine," they assured me, "we share the housework and we share Hussein, it's very convenient for all of us." They politely took turns having babies each year. I didn't want that! I wasn't putting up with that! True to my ideology, I made it a stipulation in my marriage contract that my husband could not take a second wife while he was married to me unless I agreed.

A month after my arrival we moved into our first home. We rented a semi-detached cottage in the Town of Mont Royal (TMR) with a basement for Ibrahim to see some of his patients, the rest of the week he was at the Douglas Hospital. We started the first dhikr group in Montreal. The Sufis of TMR, a disparate bunch of adventurous spirits, would go on to become the foundation of Islamic Spirituality in Canada. Our weekly dhikr became the focus of our practice, because we met together at our home, which we called the Sufi Centre. The two mosques in Montreal did not tolerate Sufi practice. The Naqshbandi is a major spiritual order of Sufism. It is the only Sufi order which connects its chain of transmission back to Abu Bakr, the first caliph of Islam and successor to Prophet Muhammad (peace be upon him). It was named after Shah Naqshband and came through Samarqand down to Damascus where it was learned by our teacher Sheikh Nazim al-Qubrusi. Sheikh Nazim gave us personal instructions and a mandate to come to Canada to help develop the Naqshbandi order. We were also orthodox Sunni Muslims following the Hanafi madhab or school of jurisprudence.

At that time the Wahabis were funding almost all the dawah, imam-training, and foundations of Islam in Canada. This puritanical and intolerant sect ruling Saudi Arabia was not recognized by many North American Muslims. According to Wahabis everything, except what they said, was "kufr, bidah or shirk"—especially Sufis, who the Wahabis claimed worshipped dead bodies. That was why they had destroyed all the graves and shrines in the Muslim world that they could, including those of the wives of Muhammad.

My first visit to the Islamic Centre of Quebec for Jumaah prayer was during a blizzard. New to winter in Quebec I didn't have an understanding of terms like "more snow," "less snow," "freezing rain," etc. To me it was all fun, a wonderful contrast to damp and dark London. So I took the bus. I figured out the change but when I waved my Montreal map with a large X marked on Grenet Street in Ville St Laurent at the driver, I think I startled him.

At that time terrorists were Irish, but Montreal's bus drivers were uniquely Quebecois and their multicultural awareness was limited. Despite my smart shalwar qameez and my tuque turban—I even spoke French: "Excusez-moi est-ce cet autobus va á la mosque?"— he was very unfriendly, and told me angrily to get to the back of the bus. Fortunately a kind-hearted woman told me when my stop was approaching.

In that incarnation, the Islamic Centre of Quebec, ICQ as it is still known, was a long, low building with a homemade minaret on top that looked like a dented crocus bulb. As women were not allowed through the front door—"AstaghfirAllah (Seek Forgiveness of Allah) sister"—I trudged through a snow bank to get round the back to a fire exit which had a "Ladies" decal on it. Someone had thoughtfully wedged a rubber slipper in it so we could get in.

Once inside, the familiar feel of wet carpeting under dry sock and a waft of curry and synthetic jasmine perfume assured me that I was in the right place. The few Muslim sisters that were there were mostly unresponsive to my enthusiastic Salaams and affectionate hand-clasping, kissing, etc. which I had learnt elsewhere. I thought I heard mumbled things about "Britishers," although one did ask "Where you are from?" I realize now that my Turkish Neo Naqshbandi hybrid and their Learned-back-home Islam were diametrically opposed. For many of the women who had bravely come to this cold distant country, Islam was marriage, children, and martyrdom, with a bit of tajweed (reciting the Quran), and samosas on special occasions. Many of them stayed home not by choice but because they simply had no idea about the way this society functioned and had no contact with the people around them. If they spoke English, they did not speak French; they had no independent income and lived in apartment buildings in dangerous areas where you had better avoid your neighbours in case you got robbed.

I was very fortunate. I had been tutored in Islam by the family of my wonderful Sheikh and now I had a fresh start from my punk post-modernist ways in the frozen wonderland of Canada. We had delicious food and lots of it, warm, well-built housing and appliances, and I also had a brilliant psychiatrist and Sufi for a husband. However, the psychic and spiritual wonders I had already witnessed, connected to traditional Islam through the shrine of Khawaja Moineddin Christi in Ajmer, India and the Naqshbandi tekke in Damascus, were radically different from that which prevailed in the close-knit and very pious Muslim community of Montreal. Perhaps these few thousand Muslims were too insecure to be tolerant at that time, but it was also the very narrow interpretation of the Sunnah of our Prophet Muhammad and restricted access to Quranic translations and interpretations that met the narrow definition of what was acceptable to the new community. A painted toenail here and a slice of Saputo cheese there and you would lose your balance on the Sirat al-Mustaqeem (Straight Path), falling into hellfire along with many other residents of Quebec.

There were "enforcers" everywhere, just like in Mecca. Usually at the mosque, but sometimes even in the segregated women's section of community meetings, they would start with a hiss. "Sister, it is my duty to tell you that your hair is showing"; or, "you closed your eyes during Salaat"; or, "your pronunciation of 'ha' is not aspirated." If they had ever got inside the Sufi Centre and seen the small photo of the Sheikh on the mantelpiece it would have been enough to send them into paroxysms of rage. "Haram! You must re-do all your prayers and face the correct qiblah (direction for praying)."

Aside from that unfortunate and vocal minority there were some wonderful and caring women. There was a genuine opening of hearts, and love and friendship were extended to me unconditionally. One of these women was the first French-Canadian woman I had ever met. She had survived a brutal upbringing in rural Quebec, escaped across Canada and after some time in Vancouver had returned to Montreal with her three-year-old daughter. When I met her she had just married a Syrian-born engineer and we were both expecting our first child as Muslim mothers. When I remember her, I see a vision of her in her newly-sewn striped jalabiya (loose gown) and a long white head scarf. She was the only woman I knew in Montreal who went freely around dressed like that. She introduced me to St Hubert Street, where we loved to shop for cheap bolts of fabric, and she gave me an English cookbook of Middle Eastern cooking. Together we looked through the English translation of Sahih hadith and Al-Ghazali's *Ihya ulum al-din* (Revival of the Religious Sciences); her husband had forbidden her to read anything else except these and *Chatelaine*. Another dear friend was born in a refugee camp in Cambodia and was only eighteen at the time she got married; she was also expecting her first baby. Later, her large son was a contrast to my small blond daughter at our dhikr meetings. We were joined by two McGill students, an American Stanford-educated girl and an Iranian man who had introduced her to Jallaluddin Rumi. There was also a tall red-haired girl from New Brunswick who had just fallen in love with a charming Tunisian man. These deep connections were made on subtle levels with hearts open to possibilities and invisible worlds of angels and miracles. Islam in North America was taking root and blossoming. What could possibly go wrong?

Our English Canadian neighbours in TMR were cool and insular. My mother-in-law referred to them as WASPs. Although technically I was also a WASP, I was never able to understand or identify with them. The large portrait of the Queen on the two-dollar bills, the brown suits, the manners and customs that had become obsolete years ago, the chemical-soaked clipped lawns. When they noticed my English accent, after I had made a point of cheerily saying Hello or Good Morning, they would exclaim . . . Ooh where are you from? Oh London, England! We were there two years ago, we went to the theatre and saw *Cats*. But noticing my Muslim gear—"Where are you really from? I mean your parents?" "Scotland and Wales?" "Your grandparents?? Oh . . . " Then they would back away totally confused. They'd heard of Jews, maybe even worked with some, and they'd heard the news reports about the Sikhs in Vancouver unfortunately, but Muslims! They were astonished that anyone would want to be like *that*; they must be so hot poor things smothered in fabric, living in cramped kitchens with no appliances, their husbands forcing them to do it all the time. The dominant image of "those women" had been on the cover of *Time*—lines of chador-clad Iranian women clutching Kalashnikovs, a picture which was ahead of its time. One hot June evening I was at the play area of the local park with my daughter, when an older, expensively suited woman cornered me under the slide. "I've been watching you." She smiled with capped teeth in a predatory sort of way, "You are very nice to that child, how much are they paying you? I'll pay you more to take care of my child . . . " When I told her she was my own daughter she looked stunned. Why would my child have blue eyes and blond hair? It was more than a cultural divide, sometimes I felt like an alien from another plant. "The Muslimah who fell to Earth."

Then there were the Quebeckers, other than my good friend in her home-made outfits. They would explain to me that although my husband was a third-generation Montrealer he was not really a Quebecer because, to use Mordecai Richler's famous phrase, he was "impure wool." On the plus side, some old men would open doors for me thinking I was a nun, and older women would curtsy and genuflect, especially when I visited St Joseph's Oratory. Looking down from the top of the Oratory over Montreal on a clear sunny day it was clear that almost everything of value had been done by Christian inclination and an army of priests and nuns. Besides, the monks still made the best cheese and had the nicest real estate. It was hard for me to understand why Montrealers backed away at the mention of religion like vampires from garlic. The division of Church and State was something I took for granted, except for the Anglican church, which didn't really count because it was founded when a sixteenth-century monarch wanted an heir. There weren't any new theocratic states spouting Islamist sound bites to terrify the population of North America and liberal Europe. The war against Islam was not on the agenda. We were living like children in a state of innocence and enthusiastic love for our new-found alternative way of living.

A year later, Ibrahim and our young family moved out to the Eastern Townships to start what we imagined would be a back to the land Sufi community. A short while later when we moved back to Montreal, I considered myself a veteran of the Canadian way of life. I had weathered a snowstorm for three days in a cabin without electricity and learnt how to plant tomatoes and watch them grow. I could walk into a halal butcher shop on Décarie and buy foul mesdames, lamb shanks, and Pataks pickles to go with them. I even had a bank account and a driver's licence! I no longer felt like an alien. I was home, safe, among friends and the vibrant Canadian Ummah.

A Muslim Woman's Perspective

AZMINA KASSAM

I WRITE FIRST AS a woman. I am a Kenya-born Canadian Muslim woman from the Shia Ismaili sect.

The Ismailis are a Muslim minority group that believes the Prophet to be the final messenger from God and that Ali, the Prophets nephew and son-in-law was the first Imam. The Aga Khan is believed by Ismailis to be the 49th descendent of Imam Ali. Through the guidance of the imams, the Ismailis have endured centuries of turbulence, persecution, and mass migrations and have come to be scattered in many parts of the world. One such exodus happened in the 1970s when Idi Amin of Uganda went on a mission to rid Uganda of all Asians including Ismailis. The unifying component of all Ismailis is the belief in the guidance of the Imam, whose prevailing advice has been to have a good education and build bridges with other communities.

As an Ismaili, there was never a question of covering my face or of wearing a hijab, but Ismailis were encouraged to dress modestly. When a close Muslim friend of mine from grade school decided to wear a full head scarf, revealing only the face, I was confused. Why would a modern Muslim woman living in a democratic society, attending a prestigious school with a western curriculum, choose this practice? Gradually I came to understanding that in the observance of her faith tradition, she felt it important to wear the head scarf even though neither her father nor her husband expected or demanded it. I believe now that the head scarf is a matter of personal choice, just as one would choose to wear a wig or a hat, though the full burqa or hijab puts severe limitations on a woman's interactions with the world.

Years later, while on a voluntary mission in Afghanistan in the mid 2000s, I felt severely inhibited in my interactions with women in full coverings. I could not read their expressions, speak to them, make eye contact. They were almost invisible and completely inaccessible to me. I felt at a deep loss that I could not communicate with my Muslim sister.

I was born in 1963, the year of Kenya's independence from the British. This was an era of great economic opportunity, growth, and prosperity. My grandfather on my father's side had little education but he had determination and ambition. He established a small bicycle shop, Nairobi Cycle Mart, that did very well. A certain British patron alerted my grandfather that he should consider getting into car spares and service and he did just that! This move proved to be most lucrative and would help to support four generations of our family. Daddy Bapa, as I fondly referred to him, owned a two-storey building that housed car parts and various accessories. He worked together with his brother and later my father, who left school at 15 years, determined to work alongside Bapa and his uncle in the shop. Daddy Bapa acquired a large property outside the city centre, on which he had custom-built a beautiful seven-bedroom house. It eventually become a home to my brother and I when many years later my mom remarried, and my brother and I both decided to move in with my father and his extended family.

My father's side of the family were highly educated. My paternal grandmother, Kursa Mama, was born to a pioneering family of eleven siblings. Her father Muhammadali Rattansi had accumulated much property in Nairobi and the neighbouring town of Nyeri. He later went on to establish a fund, The Rattansi Education Trust that still provides funding for higher learning to qualifying Kenyans. Kursa Mama had a sharp and inquisitive mind but being the eldest daughter she was expected to marry first. However, she would share with me over the years how she secretly never wanted to marry and would have loved to study further to become a doctor. She was much younger than my grandfather and had a great passion for entertaining. She would dress in beautiful saris and have her hair done in elaborate buns. She maintained a meticulous home and made magnificent flower arrangements. My grandfather indulged her. I learnt to bake cakes and made trifle puddings with her and arranged table settings. She was a voracious reader and would share her insights with me. She encouraged me to paint. She tended to lean more towards "Hindu" rituals and listened to bhajans.

From my father's side I learned about being pragmatic; the development of the intellect was highly respected and working for ones keep was a virtue. Reading and being able to converse about politics, history, the arts and other current topics were far more respected than praying before an exam and thinking you would pass because you had prayed for this.

From my mother's side of the family I learned to observe and practice the faith, to attend jamat khana which was the "gathering place" for Ismailis to worship. I would attend jamat khana regularly with my mom and grandmother. I learned the Arabic prayer and would watch my grandmother quietly roll her prayer beads reciting a zikr tasbih over and over. She was the most calming and stabilizing presence in my life and I drew strength from her inner wisdom and compassionate nature. It was her unwavering faith that gave her an inward strength and peace that had tremendous influence on me in my youth and into my life as an adult. She was clear about her role as a wife, a mother, and guardian of her large family of ten children. Mama, as I fondly referred to her, upheld a traditional system of values and family ties, and it was through her that I developed relationships with a vast group of blood relations.

My parents had separated before I was born, and I grew up among my mother's extended family. My mother was busy earning a living as a secretary. She took to badminton and went on to play in a number of championships against other clubs and against teams in neighbouring countries. At the jamat khana we would socialize after prayers with other Ismaili families and their children. The fabric of family life and community life were closely linked and we grew up knowing and seeing the same families over decades.

I attended a British-run school with a mix of South Asians, Africans, and Caucasian children. I distinctly remember singing Christian hymns, but I grew up having Christian, Hindu, and Muslim friends. I remember spending hours in our formal living room at my maternal grandparents' reading stories such as "Snow White," "Sleeping Beauty," and "Jack and the Bean Stalk." Much later, among adult books I read Simone de Beauvoir's *The Second Sex* and was fascinated by her account of the situation of women. I wrote profusely about my feelings, and writing became a way of channelling my thoughts into words and onto paper. On weekends I would go and spend time with my father. He had a love for beauty and furnished the house with Persian rugs and Chinese pottery, and he had a great marble bar built to entertain his friends with drinks. He had a deep interest in ghazals and would explain me their meanings. He believed in God but never attended jamat khana except for funerals. He had tremendous integrity and his word was his honour.

In the mid seventies my mom planned her own escape, taking me and my brother, unbeknown to my father or to us, on a flight to London, England. So began several months of being plucked out of a familiar, love-filled environment into a cold grey life of struggle and isolation. My mother rented the top part of a stone house in Muswelhill. She worked, and my brother and I changed three schools. I recall vividly turning up at school in my night slippers. It was a confusing time of uprootedness in an unfamiliar world. We left for Canada a year later.

Initially we stayed with a family, but later we moved into a co-op housing unit in Coquitlam, British Columbia. My mom found a secretarial job at a legal firm. At that time I began to act out in strange ways; I cut my eyelashes, then I began to hide food pretending to eat, but secretly I was on a mission to be as thin as possible. I got so thin that I could see my ribs and I felt this was attractive. I had my tonsils out on the pretext that I was not able to swallow food. Later I was diagnosed with a severe eating disorder, anorexia nervosa. I was shy and withdrawn in school and remember having only two friends, a Polish girl who was made fun of as a "Polack" and an Ismaili girl who had just moved to our neighbourhood. My mom sponsored my grandparents to come to Canada. Slowly I began to eat and recover a sense of control over my life. Having my grandparents with us renewed my sense of comfort and familiarity to some degree. My grandmother was very protective and kept a watchful eye over me. She did not approve of me having too many "white" friends for fear that I would pick up bad habits. My brother started smoking and hanging out after school with a group of guys. He was ashamed to be seen with us and started to resent everything related to our culture—food, language, jamat khana—struggling in his own way to create a separate identity.

I did not enjoy those years since I was teased at school; I was called "Paki" and I could not understand why. Eventually I got to high school but tended to relate more to kids from my own community. I dated an Ismaili guy from Nairobi who was struggling with his own identity as a new immigrant Ismaili Canadian man. My expectation was that I would, like everyone else, get married to a "nice Ismaili boy" in a traditional way and have a family and become a part of a large extended family where I would serve as a "dutiful daughter-in-law" and a "dutiful wife and mother."

Three years later in 1975 my mom went back to Kenya and married her childhood sweetheart. My brother went to study in England. I moved out of my grandparents' home and into a shared living arrangement with a Canadian Ismaili girl who had integrated far more than I. She introduced me to her world of diverse friendships from school and university. She was interested in politics, business, the arts, food, and wine, and travelling. We travelled together to South East Asia, Italy, and England, and she came with me to Kenya. She lived life according to her own desires and had no wish to marry. She would later struggle with her sexual identity and finally choose to be in a lesbian relationship. Our friendship, though platonic, served as an important stepping stone for each of us to pursue a life of our own choice.

My first Canadian boyfriend was another important milestone in the formation of a Canadian identity. We met at a business college in our early twenties. Guy was a real west coast guy who had a love for the sea. He introduced me to sailing, camping, cross-country skiing and hiking. He had an interest in First Nations art and introduced me to the works of Roy Vickers. We explored some of the gulf islands together. I did not mention him to my family, as I knew instinctively that this relationship would not be accepted. Though our interests aligned and we cared deeply for each other, I struggled with accepting the relationship and making it transparent within my family and community. We continued to remain friends even though our life paths diverged. I learnt from him that a healthy relationship was about each of us living out our own interests and sharing, and not imposing our values on each other. His relationship with me was always honest and transparent, and ultimately influenced my choice of life partner.

I met Arne, whose roots were Norwegian, and chose to embark on a life journey with him. Choosing this path took enormous courage from me, demanding the determination to challenge and surrender, however painful the process, a value system thickly layered in expectations, obligations, and historical ties. A system that had thus far provided a fabric of order, strength, and clarity in one's identity within a web of cultural, social, communal, and familial ties, held together by a shared history of origins, faith, persecution and multiple migrations.

My family was confused and disappointed by my decision. It opened up wounds of past family history including the failed marriage of my parents. The expectations had been that I would marry within our culture, that my marriage would strengthen old ties and bring renewal. There were issues of embarrassment and losing face in the community. I felt the voice of an entire tribe echoing with disapproval. There was confusion in my own mind as I struggled with not wanting to disappoint my family, and at the same time not wanting to go against the call of my heart. I was going against the very grain of my upbringing and taking a chance on the unknown.

I had chosen a path of significant self discovery and expansion. I chose to be with a man who resonated deeply with the Christian faith and with his identity as a Canadian.

Born in Vancouver to immigrant parents, he worked as a delivery boy for *The Sun* newspaper. Later he joined McMillan Bloedel, a big lumber company, and worked his way up the ranks. He left, to everyone's dismay, and started the Impark parking company. He would share with me later that during his Impark days he would hire many Ismaili immigrants, who had been expelled from Uganda, many of them having to start all over. He had a deep social and political conscience which would extend into many areas of committed involvements. He helped to found the Vancouver Food Bank, and he was the only member on the Board of BC Ferries who opposed the Fast Ferries. He supported many causes, including the David Suzuki Foundation, and Christianity Today, as he believed in giving a tenth of his earnings to charity. The Bible was a constant companion and he would share passages with me through our life together. One passage has always stayed with me because it spoke to me about the values which Arne lived by. It was from the Book of John: "Jesus said "Love one another as I have Loved You. "

I continued to practice my faith as an Ismaili. I attended jamat khana for regular prayers and took to practicing meditation in the early hours of the morning. I got involved in the Care for the

Elderly program and began to teach Yoga to seniors at the Ismaili Centre in Burnaby. Arne knew Bruno Fresci who was the architect who designed the Ismaili centre and he had been invited to the opening ceremony years before he met me. Sometimes Arne would attend festive occasions with me, including the occasion when the Aga Khan was visiting Vancouver and spouses were invited to meet him. He was very open and accepting of the time I gave to my faith. I felt I was connecting to an intrinsic part of me, and it was my faith that nourished me with an inner strength through Arne's illness until the time of his death.

I would go to church with Arne. I enjoyed Gospel music and the solemn sound of the organ; being inside an old church I knew I was in a sacred space. I was learning more about being Canadian, which has meant for me openness, tolerance, curiosity, and respect. It has been about engaging the other in meaningful dialogue so as to learn and expand one's understanding. It was this new life that encouraged me to go to university later in life, and soon I began a business in the area of Alternate Health and Nutrition.

The opportunity to go study at a Canadian university was an important milestone in my development. I learned to think more critically, to engage my mind on issues of gender, human rights, the environment, and civic engagement. University helped to increase my confidence. I was becoming a better informed and more engaged human being. I was able to articulate my thoughts better and had confidence and courage in sharing my opinions and disagreeing when appropriate. I also learned about Islamic civilization and the Ismaili tradition, which helped me to understand the fundamentals of my faith.

I have trouble with orthodoxies of any sort. The violence that comes from Muslim extremists is disturbing. I feel that there must be other ways to diffuse the hatred which stems from fear and the belief that all other ways are wrong.

There is a saying in the Quran which speaks to me more now than ever, when I try to understand the wars and all the unnecessary killing of innocent lives. Surah 49:13 says:

> O mankind! We created you from a single (pair) of
> a male and a female, and made you into nations and
> tribes, that ye may know each other (not that ye may
> despise (each other). Verily the most honoured of you
> in the sight of Allah is (he who is) the most righteous
> of you. And Allah has full knowledge and is well
> acquainted (with all things).

The evolution of my identity as an Ismaili-Muslim Kenyan
Canadian has involved many influences. I feel I am a construct of
multiple identities which are fluid and still in the process of construction. I am a part of a nation that by its very nature is expansive,
multicultural, and diverse. Having had the courage and support
to expand out of the familiar into the unknown has been deeply
satisfying.

Muslim Me

MARIA CRUZ

HI, SALAAM. I'M MARIA. If you see me on the street I'll bet you won't be able to miss me. I have a buzz cut that's *really* short when I first get it done—yeah, in the winter I don't have as much built-in insulation up top, but it feels great and it's easy to manage. Since I'm blind I use a white cane, and since I'm also physically disabled I use a power wheelchair too.

I wear jeans, sweatpants, or dress pants. You definitely won't see me in a skirt or dress. When I tried wearing that femmie stuff, it was too hard for me to manage, and it was never my style anyway. In the summer I wear crewneck T-shirts, or maybe a dressier crewneck sweater or polo top, but I still wear long pants instead of shorts. So if you see a package like me coming at you, what would you think about me? Some people think I'm a guy. Some people may think I'm a lesbian. Some people seem to think someone forced me to look this way. Some people may not think anything at all. But would anyone think, "She's a Muslim"?

Sometimes I'm glad people don't know I'm Muslim. I cuss way too much, especially when I'm having a lot of trouble doing stuff, and that's most of the time. I figure with my anger management issues I'm not exactly a good example of a good Muslim, and I don't want people to think badly of other Muslims because of the crap I can't seem to keep from spewing out of my mouth. In fact, I often don't mention to people that I'm Muslim unless it comes up in a conversation. Although when I do mention it, the other person either sounds happy or excited, or sometimes a little surprised.

But there are other times when I wish people knew I was Muslim, because it might help them realize there's more than one way for a Muslim sister to look, or act, or be. I think a lot of people see Muslim sisters as quiet, subdued women in burqas and hijabs, with little or no education and terrorist leanings. Yes, some of us wear burqas, but lots of us dress in different ways. Some of us wear hijabs, but lots of us don't.

Personally I think it should be a woman's choice whether to wear a hijab or not, and I don't think my bare, buzzed head makes me immodest. Yes, some of us are quiet and subdued, but definitely not all of us. In fact, we're not all tied to submissive men either, or any man for that matter. For example, I've never been married, or even found anyone I'm interested in, and I'm perfectly happy to stay single if I don't find that special someone. I think any marriage should be an equal partnership with each spouse taking on the roles that suit her or his abilities, strengths and personality. I don't believe men should have control over women and I think any man who abuses a woman should either be forced into treatment or be put in jail.

Muslim women may not all be well educated, but many of us have university degrees. I went to the University of Toronto but didn't get a degree, since my disabilities and financial situation made it impossible for me to get past the second year. I think everyone should have access to the education they want, no matter what their financial situation, disability, gender or religion are. But I'm sure I'm only one of many Muslim women who try to educate ourselves even though we can't access a university education. And although some of us are unfortunately misguided enough to agree with the terrorists, many more of us condemn terrorism and the acts terrorists commit.

I'm definitely for people fighting against oppression, as long as the way they fight doesn't oppress someone else. Killing innocent people, destroying schools, kidnapping and rape are all acts committed by low-life scumbags who aren't freedom-fighters but criminals who need to be put away. The way to end oppression isn't to make other people suffer, and the so-called Muslims who commit terrorism aren't practicing Islam the way it was meant to be practiced.

Speaking of terrorism, I need to add something else here. A lot of people seem to use the word "jihad" in relation to terrorism. From what I was taught, jihad means struggle, and this means internal struggle as much as external conflict. It's not supposed to mean the kind of crap that's being perpetrated by groups like ISIS/ISIL, Boko Haram, etc. For me jihad can mean struggling against oppression, as long as I'm not oppressing someone else to do that. But to me jihad also means my own internal struggle to do as much good as possible in my life.

Maybe you're wondering how I got to be the quirky, strong-willed person I am. Well, there's nothing specific that made me the way I am; in fact I've been a nonconformist loner from the beginning, even though as a kid I didn't have much of a chance or means to express myself. I was adopted by a Canadian family who I think is mostly Christian and white, and although I couldn't really see what anyone looked like, I grew up not feeling I fitted in with them. I always wondered about my background, and when I was little I asked them what I was, to which they answered, "You're a human being" (which actually was a pretty good answer). I have memories (or at least what I'm pretty sure are real memories) of being a baby and hearing mostly New York City or New Jersey accents, and I've always had the very strong feeling I was Puerto Rican.

I didn't grow up wishing I was from New York or New Jersey, or wishing I was Puerto Rican, or anything like that, it's just a strong gut feeling I've always had. And when I remembered the people I thought might have been my birth parents, I also had a feeling they were Muslim, although there's nothing specific I can put my finger on to make me think this. That's not the main reason I became Muslim though, the snippets I learned about Islam over the years just made more sense to me than other religious stuff I heard.

Yet when I tried to find my birth information as an adult, nothing matched up with what I remembered. I even met my birth mom (who I'm told is Canadian and white), and I asked the poor woman lots of questions like, "Were you ever in New York or New Jersey when you were pregnant with me?" and "Is anyone in your family Puerto Rican?" etc. I love her and think she's a great person and I would never want to hurt her; but nothing added up for me. Although I can tell my skin colour is light, I don't have enough sight to see what my facial features look like and I've never really thought of myself as having a Canadian identity because I've never really felt at home in Canada. I've always considered New York to be home even though I've only been there a couple of times as an adult, and before then I was only there as a baby (if my memories are correct).

Although I was born with both my disabilities, my neurological conditions weren't diagnosed when I was a kid, as far as I know. People knew I had low vision but everyone seemed to think I had a lot more sight than I really had, so I wasn't given the nonvisual clues I needed to know what was around me or what was going on. It was really hard for me to read the large print I was given in school, and I was never given the choice to learn Braille or have materials read aloud on tape. So the only way I got through school with even half-decent marks was by listening to the teachers and using my wits.

As for my physical disability, people seemed to think that I was just clumsy or lazy and just needed more exercise, when the reality was that I couldn't do any more than I was doing, especially since I had no mobility aids or other stuff to help me get around and do things easier. As a kid I was always told to hurry up and that I was too slow. This made me mad not only because I was already going as fast as I could, but also because I'd always wanted to be able to move fast and couldn't.

I've never been much of a talker, partly because speaking is physically tiring for me and partly because I have trouble finding the right words. As a kid it was even worse, because my vocabulary wasn't as developed as most other kids' vocabulary, and I'm sad to say I probably hurt some people with the words that came out when I didn't have the right words. The messed-up thing was, I had absolutely no idea that the words I was saying were horrible and hurtful, and people didn't usually tell me they were. But at least now I'm pretty good at putting my thoughts down into a computer, as long as I have enough time to do it. And eating was always a major chore for me, never really a pleasure, because I also have chewing and swallowing difficulties that make it hard to eat food that's fibrous or pulpy, or food that's mixed together, such as stews and soups.

Growing up I was always expected to do stuff I couldn't do, and because I hardly knew anything about my disabilities I didn't know why I couldn't do what people wanted me to do. So I just thought I was no-good and couldn't do anything right, without knowing why. I've always felt like a weirdo whether I'm with Muslim, non-Muslim, disabled or able-bodied people, so I have to just do what works for me and what I think is right.

Being a Muslim with my disabilities is a struggle too, since it's very hard for me to do ablution and even praying is physically tiring for me. I pray five times a day (or at least try to), and do dhikr (remembrance of God), and even pray to God informally throughout the day (although I'm afraid my informal prayers are usually more like rants). So Islam's a big part of my life. But I don't consider myself to be capital-R religious. What I mean is that I'm mostly thinking about trying to do the best I can with what I've got, and trying to help other people as much as I can.

I guess I'm not comfortable with formality, and my disabilities also make it hard to do a lot of the routine stuff we Muslims do. I'm nonsectarian, so I'm not Sunni, Shia, Sufi, etc. Some Muslims believe we should have Sharia law, but I don't believe we should. I think we should adhere to the laws of whatever country we live in. Yes, we should be able to have halal stuff, and wear whatever clothing we feel fits with our religious beliefs as long as it's clothing we choose and not what someone forces us to wear. But I don't think we need Sharia to be good Muslims. In fact, people seem to have so many different ways of interpreting the Quran, some of these being really oppressive, that I think it would be really hard to implement Sharia law in a completely just way. No legal structure is perfect, of course, since they're implemented by human beings, and none of us is perfect.

I think God just hardwired me to be the stubborn nonconformist I am to help me push through all the crap. For example, since I was little I've always wanted to be a cop so I can put away really nasty people (like rapists, kidnappers, abusers and murderers). I'm sure if I'd been born sighted and able-bodied I would have been a cop, or maybe an engineer, or maybe even both. But although it still bugs me that I can't be a cop, I try to find other stuff I can do to make a positive difference in the world. I do web design (which wasn't hardwired in me), and I taught myself to do this by finding online tutorials that helped me learn some web coding languages and web accessibility standards. Although I have my own web design business, I only have a couple of clients, and not only have I never made any profit but I also got myself deeper into debt. But I try to make sure every site I design is accessible for everyone, including people with disabilities.

When I have the energy I also try to help improve accessibility for other websites, e-mailing companies or organizations about accessibility problems I had using their site and giving them information about how to fix them. I do some other activist and advocacy stuff here and there, not just around accessibility issues but also around other issues I think are important. I also volunteer in other ways, like helping to design assistive devices for people with disabilities. I still haven't found my niche, and I'm trying to find something I can do to really help other people and myself. But Inshallah (God willing) I'll find it soon.

Brackish Water

YASMINE MALLICK

IT'S BEEN TEN YEARS. I write this as my husband sleeps, warmly nestled next to me. He hasn't read this. He knows about my illness. Ignoring my family's pleas to keep quiet, it was one of the first things I told him about when we started talking. But I spared him the details of how I had tried to take my own life and about the sexual assaults that never seemed to cease. I think he would break if I told him those. I run my fingers through the soft hair near the nape of his neck. I love him, achingly.

My grandmother used to go into the bazaar in Dhaka and take off her gold bangles one by one, and give them out to the poor and destitute on the street. She would return from her philanthropy and curse at anyone who came her way. Unexplainable shifts in mood. At the end of her life she had managed to alienate almost everyone in our family. She had lain in bed all day, unable to move. No one ever told me about that. If I had known about her, could I have saved myself?

Mental illness can touch anyone. It does not discriminate. My hijab or praying five times a day did not make me immune. Our Blessed Prophet (peace be upon him) said: "The Pen is lifted from three [i.e., their deeds are not recorded]: a child until he reaches puberty; an insane man until he comes to his senses; one who is asleep until he wakes up" (Abu Dawud 4403 and Ibn Majah 2041).

My Lord would never hold me to account for things that were out of my hands. If only people could live by that kind of justice.

Psychosis shatters the barrier between your dreaming and waking worlds. Your nightmares come to life. It is awe-inspiring, exhilarating, and utterly frightening. When that thread snapped in me, I caught a brief glimpse into a world of raw surreal beauty. This is something I am still struggling to comprehend.

For someone who had placed all her trust in her intellect, the loss of my mind left me shattered. But in that utter obliteration, somehow with God's grace, I healed and revived. There is triumph there. And we are all capable of it. As Ibn Al Qayyim said, "When a diver sinks into the sea, he collects pearls and then rises again."

My husband stirs in his sleep. I shut the laptop and burrow into the covers beside him. Spending a lifetime unmoored in the brackish waters, she finally drops anchor.

A Family Vacation: Egypt, Aboard a Cruise Ship on the Nile

She faces the Kush ruins, barefoot on the starboard AstroTurf. These remnants of ancient Nubia have no interest for the other tourists. The crumbling mud walls are anticlimactic after the Valley of the Kings and the tomb of Tutankhamun. But she likes the Kushite decay— more humble, organic, raw, and real. The wind blusters around her as she stands there at the edge, but she is at peace. She prayed at dawn on the fake grass amid the plastic lawn chairs and now, as she watches the rising sun, she feels she understands. She knows she lived in those mud fortresses on the shore long ago, when the clay of her body was still part of the bedrock, swimming and mingling in the river delta.

Cairo, at the Dock

They hold a festive cruise buffet heralding in the New Year. Falafel, tabouleh, grape leaves piled high, shrimp bisque, and biryani—a gustatory smorgasbord of delight. The belly dancers are set loose. Their rhythmic, undulating fleshy bodies are intoxicating, even more tantalizing in their costumes of naked iridescent shimmer. Two young girls sit on the floor and clap with the beat. The most beautiful dancer comes thrillingly close. She quivers to the Egyptian drumbeat. The light catches the fine layer of sweat that sheaths her body. Both girls, as they sit in the dark looking up at this leggy wonder, have never been more utterly seduced.

The whirling dervishes are unleashed. They are utterly hypnotic, whirling cloth—masculine torsos. The two girls clap with the music. Forgotten underneath the tablecloth, they like the safety of the darkness, the anonymity. Here, the little girl doesn't have to feel like an outcast. And the older one can, for a while, forget.

Cairo, at the Hotel

It is 2 AM Her father rings the bell at the desk and waits wearily. The hotel lobby is spectacular. The ten-foot Christmas tree, decadent in all it's red and gold splendor, towers over her. She inspects the jewelry in the glass showcases and picks out a massive rainbow-gemmed paisley. Her father returns and they begin their trek outside to the villas. She has always loved walking in grass fields at night, and this field in Egypt, with its series of mirage-like blue ponds and bridges, is breathtaking. They follow the bellhop in a single file: her father, mother, and two younger sisters. She lingers behind, throws her head back, and drinks in the stars.

Because Christmas music plays on the hotel intercom endlessly, she sings Wham's "Last Christmas" and hops around the suite. Her sisters stare at her in amazement but laugh. She gives her youngest sister a back massage with the hotel lotion, and the little girl falls asleep under her hands. It is perhaps 4 AM, and both her sisters are nestled deeply inside the plush comforters. Too wired to sleep, she takes a shower in the glistening white porcelain bathroom. The phone rings. "Assalamu-'alaikum," the man at the front desk drones, "It is time for *fajr* prayer." She thanks him, hangs up, and returns to her shower. Later, the three sisters pray as the pink sun begins to bleed along the horizon. Through the terrace window, they watch the indigo and salmon commingle above the dark verdant grass fields. A watercolor painted just for them.

Edfu, the Temple of Horus

The gold sand-drenched temple walls are overwhelming. The tour guide, Qaseem, smiles at her as he recounts how Horus fought the God of Chaos here and won. She understands the hieroglyphics now. The gaping mouths become eyes and then loaves of bread—the letter R, for the sun god Ra. The letter F—the horned viper molts and morphs into a slug and then transforms again into a snake, a *naga*.

Parts of the orchestra's score have become inharmonious and incomprehensible. The brass section bruises the woodwinds in their onslaught. The strings strangle the percussion. Ancient Egyptian melds with Hindi; Somalia and Nubia merge; and they all become a part of her.

In the gift shop, she fingers all the obelisks of translucent alabaster and impervious black marble. A young man greets her with "Assalamu-'alaikum," and though inappropriate, he takes her hand warmly. He is handsome, and she beams. In her hand, he leaves a tiny scarab made of turquoise. He pursues her through the entire store. She is afraid now. He catches her hand again and presses another blue scarab in her palm. She collects four scarabs by the end of the shopping trip and places them all back on one of the shelves. She hurriedly tries to follow the rest of the group back to the tour bus. He grabs her hand again. "How about one kiss?"

"I can't. I really have to go."

He crushes every bone in her hand. "Just one, to say goodbye. We'll go behind the pillar."

She tears her hand away, "No!" and runs back to the bus.

Onboard the Cruise Ship

It is Christmas Eve. As the rest of the ship feasts and dances, she wanders up the stairs to the deck. The ship is anchored in the middle of the river next to another liner. The guide told them the group would be allowed to ship-hop and attend the other cruise's parties. She takes off her Nikes and walks on the prickly astroturf. She tiptoes around the pool edge and on to the ledge of the ship itself. The river roars beneath her, violently bashing up against the ship's stern. She imagines what it would be like to fall into these waters on this dark night, as everyone gets drunk on the deck below her. If she jumped, she thinks, the water would crush her into fine dust.

Outside El-Nozha Airport, Alexandria

The family waits for a cab, bleary-eyed after their flight. Mahmood bounds towards them, offering his car. All five climb into the taxi as Mahmood loads their luggage in the trunk. They roll over potholes and narrowly escape a roadside ditch. Massive truck tires appear on the road out of nowhere. The high beams are blown out, and they barely manage to veer out of the way. Her father grips onto the edge of the window, knuckles turning yellow. The car stops. Mahmood and her father get out and start pushing, but the engine won't start. Mahmood calls up one of his cabbie friends, and he arrives and takes the family the rest of the way to Alexandria. The oldest daughter sits in the back, shuts her eyes, and wills herself into a corpse state. She feels herself rising out of her body. She is flanked by her sister and mother. Every time the car lurches, they grip her arm from either side. Her soul stops rising and returns.

Cairo, Aboard the Cruise Ship

They board the ship carrying their tons of luggage. The three girls get a room across the hall from their parents. They start filling the drawers and cupboards with their knick-knacks. The oldest one plays with the dials of a mysterious contraption she finds in between the two beds. The writing has worn away. After hours of experimenting, she discovers that the tiniest knob on the right actually adjusts the static on the TV, the intercom area connects to the front desk, but the large knob in the middle still remains elusive.

She stares at the only intelligible channel she has managed to find with an English news feed crawling along the bottom. The news is garbled. She has to learn how to quickly filter out the lies from the half-truths. She turns a dial and the program takes her to the 1960s. She presses another button and it takes her five years into the future. The screen abruptly flashes and dissolves. In that brief second she sees a subliminal image of Ra on his night journey through the underworld. She is hit with a sudden feeling of thirst. She tilts her head back and water drizzles from Ra's staff into her open mouth. It tastes like tangerines.

Luxor

The tour guide leads the group through an immaculate garden into a store. The tourists sit in two rows of chairs facing each other. Soon a salesman walks in and launches into a history of perfume oils and incense in Egypt. Young women cloaked in full abayas and niqab breeze through the group, dabbing and dousing all the eager customers with 'attar. They move in a cloud of peppermint, lavender, bergamot, and mint. The tourists leave reeking of myrrh, frankincense, Egyptian geranium, and sandalwood, weighed down with shopping bags full of perfumes and incense. They return through the same garden, where geraniums keep blooming, the mint leaves curl up to the sun, and the scent of lavender lies heavy in the humid desert air.

Aboard the Cruise Ship on the Nile

Muntaser leers at her hungrily over the counter. Oblivious, she continues to browse. She likes this tiny cramped gold *souq* in the ship. The engraved hieroglyphics are bewitching. She wants to look as in a museum. Muntaser leans in. "I liked how you danced." He shakes his body lewdly to some imagined beat. "What do you do up on the ship's deck at night?" He eyes her eagerly.

Something breaks inside her. In hurried half-English, half-Arabic, she tries to explain. "I pray up on the deck. *Salaatul-fajr.*" She starts to cry and Muntaser is horrified. He nods, trying to erase everything that was said. Realizing he can't, he apologizes profusely.

Later, a man comes into Muntaser's shop and orders three gold pendants, to be engraved with his daughters' names in hieroglyphics. Though he hasn't been asked, Muntaser painstakingly carves on the back of one of the daughters' *kartoushes*, the same young girl that cried in front of him that day. He etches the entire hieroglyphic alphabet into the soft gold. The letters flash as he mutters a prayer for her to ward off the evil eye.

Aswan, at the Train Station

The whistle of a distant train screams in the wind as the tour group waits for their car number. The oldest daughter needs to go the bathroom and finds a dilapidated one beside a cluster of shops. The cleaning woman sits there. Knowing she expects a tip, the girl fumbles around in her pockets and produces a tiny bar of hotel soap. She gives this to the lady. The washerwoman breaks into a gold-toothed grin and pulls her into a hearty embrace. Still warm from the hug, the daughter makes her way back to her family. Their train car has arrived, and they go aboard.

She shares a room with her youngest sister. The entire family has contracted some kind of traveller's sickness. The little girl vomits into the wool blanket and her older sister spends the night nursing her until she falls asleep again. The room has a bunk bed and a whole series of interconnected compartments. Like Chinese boxes, every cabinet opens into another. The oldest sister finds this enchanting. In the cabinet mirror she stares at the gray face that looks back at her in the half light. Her lip is gashed where he kissed her, and she still hasn't managed to stop the bleeding. She carefully applies some cream to the wound. As the train roars ahead on the tracks, she watches Aswan go by. She presses her face against the cold glass of the little window, trying to make something out in the darkness, and prays.

Aboard the Cruise Ship

They hold a masquerade ball on New Year's Eve. Bent over a mahogany table, she sits engrossed, playing chess with a little boy. He's very intelligent and loves astrophysics, abstract philosophy, and fractals, just like she does. He is amused that she has no strategy in her game, and it is this that makes her an exciting opponent. It is nearing midnight. The waiters pass by wearing ghastly theatre masks. Later, the same two waiters pass by again and beckon for them to join the party in the next room. Both chess players shudder and refuse.

Pawn to knight.

Time stops.

In this web of déjà vu, she has lost herself. Time is a wholly human construct, and she thinks that if she doesn't attend the ball, the world will remain as silent and frozen as it is now.

She wonders what it would be like to kiss the intense boy sitting across from her. Would he change? Would she?

The noisemakers and whistles sound. The clock chimes midnight. The spell is broken. The waiters continue merrymaking. The rewind button is released.

She feels the bath water go inside of her and prays that it takes away the impression of his fingers when he clutched her between her legs. This can be washed away. She believes this with conviction and scrubs until her skin is aching and raw.

The waters envelop her in a turbid wave of black ice and fear.

He grabs her hand. She is crying now. Her little sister watches in horror, sobbing. She had only wanted to console him. He seemed so beaten as he sat in his tiny store in the hotel. A broken soldier who had lost everything. He had told her his life story; how when he came back after the war, he lost the woman he had loved. When she asked what her name was, he replied with her own. This was jarring. But somehow it seemed fitting. She paid for the crystal *tasbih*, emptying out her wallet. A parting gift for her mother. She had wanted to give him a goodbye hug, just to show she cared, and he had grabbed her then.

He is at least eighty years old. With his rotting teeth he bites into her lip with desire, sliding his insidious, slippery tongue into her mouth. They are in the ship's bunker. Cockroaches crawl over the tea cups. She looks out onto the waters at the ship's helm and sees Makkah. She is performing her last sacred rites. This has happened seven times before, like the seven circumambulations around the Ka'bah. She has traversed the distance between Safa and Marwah seven times as well.

White marble floor/his hands on her body/water/death.

She chooses her words carefully. "No, I wasn't raped. It didn't go that far. But I believed I had been." Already expecting this response, the nurse nods vigorously, "Yes, you were delusional. It's part of your illness." The nurse says this matter-of-factly, carelessly, as if she knows. The girl shuts her eyes and wills her to leave. The nurse takes the subliminal order, and the door clicks shut as she marches out. The girl wearily rakes her fingers through her hair. It has been shorn violently, the aftermath of when she donned her Japanese robe and performed a ceremonial suicide over the bathroom sink. The edges are jagged and broken, like how she feels inside.

The dense aroma of the star gazers suffocates the room. A gift from her guilt-ridden "boyfriend," the one who has given up and stopped trying to understand her. From then on, she will always hate the scent of lilies. The turmeric-stained stamens will forever remind her of antiseptic and death. Using the oil pastels that he's left behind, she rubs the colours into her fingers and draws the desolate tree outside her window. She turns the white pine into a Japanese *sakura*. Black bark bearing blossom, lemon and gray sky. He comes by the following day, sits on the edge of her hospital bed, and they draw together. Holding her *sakura*, confused, he asks, "But where are the leaves?"

She crosses seven bridges to reach the ship. Seven—like the number of heavens.

She is hurtling recklessly through the streets on an open-carriage ride with her parents. The Kodak film store rushes past. Yellow. They pass a train station. Pink. Then a *souq*. Orange. It is all spherical. A spinning colour wheel. All she had to do was take one more step, and the thin membrane that held everything together, ruptured. As the yolk bleeds, everything coalesces, merges, then melds, and disintegrates. In the aftershock, the ground reverberates, and what resounds clearly is this: this is it. The moment. There will never be any other.

She must rid herself of everything. Become the nomad she has always been. Discard her backpack and spend all her money. It is time.

She picks the tiniest ornament from the Christmas tree. Opening the wrapping, she finds a Styrofoam box. Perfect. It weighs nothing.

She takes off her necklace and leaves it hanging on the banister. Next off comes her cardigan. She can't remember where or when she took off her hijab. She feels as light as a thistledown seed in the wind. She floats up the stairs to a luxuriously decorated room. Animal skin rugs on the floor and brocaded silk couches. She crawls under the sofa. No one will ever find her.

The terrace door blows open. She hears the wind beckoning and follows it outside. There on the balcony, only in this silence, she hears the violin and cello wailing while the waters crash upon the surf. She climbs onto the ledge overlooking the turquoise ponds.

The wind rushes through the date palms.

"Take me now, Lord. I am ready," she whispers.

This is her solo. And she has failed.

The cymbals crash—the grand finale.

She does not jump.

Instead, she remains on the brink. She never knew sanity could be so fragile, that everything could fracture so horribly and irrevocably. That survival could be such triumph. She breaks the surface of the brackish black obsidian. She is bruised, and although her lungs are waterlogged, she breathes.

Welcome to Toronto

MONA HASHIM

I CAN NEVER FORGET that day, ten years ago. On the way from the airport to our new home in Toronto, I was amazed by the wide roads, tall buildings, and the diverse population. Coming from Egypt to Toronto had been difficult, I recalled my mom's face in Cairo and had said good bye to my sister at the airport. The first leg of the journey, from Cairo to Italy, had been short. During the second leg we saw a lot of turbulence. For almost an hour the plane was jumping up and down like a child. Some passengers started to scream, others were in tears. I was thankful to Allah that my kids were sleeping. But I felt we would not make it. I took out my little Quran and I started to read some verses loudly. Thoughts of my mother receiving the sad news crammed my mind and the salty taste of my own tears filled my mouth. Suddenly, the aircraft started to land and all the terrible feelings disappeared. During the third leg, I found myself in a huge 747 jet crowded with passengers from South Asia. There were infants who didn't stop crying, a little boy who was crawling on the floor, and a strong smell of spicy food. My kids woke up happily, watched some films, and ate their meals.

My first few days in Toronto were busy with official papers and settling down. We came to Canada because my husband was offered a job; we planned to stay for a few years and then go back home. However, as the nice Palestinian girl who sat next to me said, "Once you are stuck here, it will be difficult to go back." Twice every day I had to walk my kids to school and bring them back. Though the day looked busy, my soul seemed empty and I felt deeply isolated. Calling home through the internet was not an option then. My husband had to work hard, even during weekends. I had to face many challenges all by myself.

I lived in an area that was crowded with people of Asian origin; although most of the residents shared the same culture and religion, I was lonely. There were few families of Arabic origin that we used to see occasionally. It took another year before I got involved in their regular meetings. Throughout the first eight years of my life, I dedicated myself to raising my kids. But with them growing up, the eagerness and passion to continue my dream had gone away. I brought my degree and my certificates with me along with my work permit. To my surprise, I found that all the settlement and employment services were dedicated to immigrants. I wasn't able to join any English program and I wasn't eligible to get any help to be employed. Finally I heard the magic word that gave a new meaning to my life: volunteering. I applied to volunteer at my kids' school and had the first interview in my life. I was then able to help the class teacher for a couple of hours, two days a week.

Volunteering in my kids' elementary and middle schools and at the downtown hospital filled the emptiness in my soul. When summer approached, I fell in love with the flourishing parks. All this beauty was for free; back home we used to pay money to enjoy a peaceful day. The second Canadian winter was the time for us to revisit our future plans. It was very obvious that Toronto was different from Amsterdam, where we had lived; that scary feeling of being a stranger was not there because everyone in Canada is an immigrant and the only people who can claim this land as truly theirs are unfortunately suppressed.

We were in Amsterdam in 2001 when the 9/11 attacks happened. I recall when my husband called us, sounding serious, and told us to turn on the TV. The following day outside my kids' school, parents were gathered in circles and from time to time would look at me. I picked up my kids and left quickly. I have to admit that throughout my ten years in Toronto, I always felt welcome wherever I went. People helped me to get my shopping cart to the bus, guided me through the downtown streets. Once, on a dark and cold Christmas eve, a nice bus driver pointed out to us the mosque in Scarborough. Of course there were a few incidents where I was called names and had the middle finger raised at me. But generally speaking, I didn't feel like a stranger.

My husband reached the conclusion that we should apply to be immigrants. It was a long process of a few years, during which I was fortunate to study some courses, and was offered my first full-time job. A new stage in my life began. Even though the first four years were tough, we also had fun. We went to Niagara Falls, and we learned skating; not to mention the family tradition we created . . . camping! One day my husband suggested that in Canada we should do what the Canadians do. Camping is not familiar in our culture, I remember the funny smiles that we got from our Arabic friends when we suggested we go camping together. We found camping site in the provincial park near Guelph. Putting up a tent was not as easy as we thought; arranging our food and equipment was our next step. By the time we had everything done, I was exhausted, my husband was tired, and the kids were confused, having expected more fun.

Darkness swiftly made its way through the camp area. The leaves and the branches looked like ghosts in the heavy silence surrounding the tent. We washed ourselves and brushed our teeth. We put a huge plastic table cloth and performed our night prayer; I was never touched by prayer as I did that night. All the creatures that we could see and those we could not were listening.

I decided to study employment counselling at one of the colleges. This was a very stressful time in my life, when I had to study and take care of the home and my kids for one whole year.

I remember those long days when I came home at night to follow up with the kids and with my home chores. There were many times when I fell asleep while helping the kids with their homework. I recall one night in September 2011 when I was ready to quit. I am glad I didn't, and fought my battle to its end. Though I graduated with honours, I missed my family during my graduation ceremony. I wanted to tell my father that his daughter had a degree from a Canadian college. My father died before seeing his hopes of me come to reality.

During my school years when I was younger, my family and my teachers expected a bright future for me; I turned those dreams down for the sake of the man I had married. I stayed home for eight years to take care of our kids. I am not regretting those years, but during that phase in my life, my self confidence went away.

I had my first job contract six months after ending my studies. Though the location of the job was far, I had no choice but to accept it. Jobs within my career were scarce, and half my colleagues were desperately searching. I have now worked for many organizations and counselled people from various cultures and backgrounds. My work is difficult, as I am required to meet quotas. But how can the life of a human being be translated into a number to be added to my monthly report? The best moments are when a client leaves my office with a grateful smile or calls me on the phone to thank me. I might have tears in my eyes when a client gives me a hug and shakes my hand with gratitude. Helping people is amazing, especially when it's a Muslim woman with a long dress and a scarf, who prays at her workplace and fasts during Ramadan, who's doing it.

I used to say that Canada is much better than the US. However, in the last few years, as an observing Muslim woman wearing the scarf I am getting a different message. I voted in the elections for the first time in my life. Back in Egypt, I didn't care to vote because the elections were a fraud. Our presidents would remain until they either died or were killed! Voting is an essential right, people die in other parts of the world because they want to vote. That's why the people in Egypt decided it was time for a change. They wanted their voices to be heard. In January 2011, I heard the news of the angry demonstrations that filled Tahreer square in Cairo. I was delighted when Mubarak's regime was overthrown. The country had lived with corruption, abuse, and torture for the last fifty years. For the first time I felt proud to be an Egyptian.

With the first elected president Dr Mohamed Morsi, my hopes rose high. Sadly, only a year later, the hidden fingers that shaped the destiny of our world played their role and the president was opted out and the country entered a dark military era. There followed a massacre of more than 3000 innocent people who protested. As a Canadian Egyptian, I feel sad that Canada is supporting the military coup in Egypt.

Ten years ago, I planned to come for a few years and go back. Then I began to feel that Canada was my home. I'm not sure anymore if I feel safe here. What will the future be for my kids? The talk about the hijab and niqab and the overall Islamophobia that has grown makes the future seem uncertain. Canada gave me freedom, but now things are changing. Will I have to give up my ethics? My identity as a Muslim? I would like to be treated as a Canadian, because I know that being Canadian is about accepting our differences.

A Matter of Prayer

MARIAM HAMAOUI

MY STORY BEGINS in two countries half a world away, one with a history of war, the other currently writing its history of a war. I was born to Lebanese and Syrian parents. My parents eventually divorced, but both remarried. I am one of eight children, with three sisters and four brothers. I speak English and Arabic and am currently in the process of learning French. I am a Muslim woman, and was taught the faith by my father, who never strictly imposed it but rather allowed me to learn it my own way. For that I have always been grateful.

I began to study Religious Studies at York University in 2010. My love for religion developed in my Grade 11 "World Religions" class in high school. Dr Smith, my teacher at the time, liked to challenge my views about religion. In hindsight I now see how that allowed me to open my mind and expand my horizons. There were about three other Muslim students in the class, but they were not fond of his approach and dropped the class, perhaps fearing that their faith would be shaken. I found the class intriguing; I enjoyed the challenge and valued the learning experience. To make sure I was paying attention, I would always sit in the front of the class.

I believe religion needs to be studied, debated, and critiqued in order to find the right answers. This belief is a result of the environment I grew up in. Both my father and my teacher did what others could not do, teach. Dr Smith encouraged students to debate and challenge each other. He made us look outside the box, outside what was taught at home or at the religious institutions or religious schools we attended. He wanted to teach us to use our own minds, and to come to our own conclusions.

Earlier in my high school days, being an Arab Muslim was in its own way a disadvantage. When I was in Grade 10, my English teacher taught us in the beginning of the year not to say God's name. "Do not say 'Oh my God,' how would you like it if I said 'Oh my Allah'?" And that was only the beginning. This same teacher was failing me. I approached her to find out why I was failing, and she responded by saying, "because of cultural reasons." I was appalled. What did she mean? Was it that I'm of Arab background? What did that have to do with anything? I was born in Canada, why does my culture matter? Was it because of my religious belief? How could being a Muslim affect my grade?

I asked her to explain what she meant. She said she had to leave to go to her next class. I refused to leave without a detailed answer. I was distraught and angered by the way I was being treated. A friend of mine stood beside me, as I challenged the teacher. She had a trolley and kept pushing it against my friend's feet in order for her to move. She walked over to the PA system and told the secretary to send the security guard to the third floor due to two students harassing her. I did not wait but walked to the office to speak with the vice-principal. On my way there I passed by the security guard who had been sent to speak to me. The vice-principal, who was of Egyptian background, was also curious why I would receive a failing mark due to "cultural reasons." I explained the situation to him and arranged to have my parents come to the school to speak to the teacher.

The teacher apologized and said that Arabs and Muslims don't understand Shakespeare. From what she understood, Shakespeare was not taught in that part of the world and that I would naturally not understand Shakespeare due to the cultural environment I grew up in. My parents right away corrected her ignorance by telling her that Shakespeare is taught in the Middle East. At the end of the year, I passed with a 50% in the course. I didn't fail but I didn't learn much. Instead of trying to teach me Shakespeare the teacher had stereotyped me and thought me a lost cause from the onset.

When I got accepted at York University for Religious Studies, I attended with the aim of furthering my understanding of world religions. I looked for any sort of organization to join on campus. I wanted to make a difference. I decided to start with what I already knew, being involved in sports. This came across my mind since I was heavily involved in managing and part of sport teams in high school. But I wanted something different. I joined the Student Council of Liberal Arts and Professional Studies as a counsellor. Then I co-founded one of the largest student clubs on campus, the Middle Eastern Students' Association. This was the start of my activism.

In my second year of university, I became the vice-president of the Middle Eastern Students' Association. Because of my involvement and leadership in the community, a friend of mine informed me of an increasing number of complaints that had been directed at the Toronto District School Board (TDSB) for allowing elementary-school children to practice their prayers. Every Friday, young students would gather to pray at the Valley Park Middle School. Complaints were followed by rallies and protests. The rationale behind using the cafeteria, at a time when it was not in any other use, was that students would no longer need to walk over two blocks to the closest mosque. Rather than lose a significant chunk of their afternoon, using the cafeteria would allow them to miss as little class time as possible. This was also the safest option for them, since they would not have to walk on the streets unsupervised.

I attended a rally in front of the TDSB headquarters in North York on July 25, 2011, with a friend of mine who made the decision to wear the head scarf that very day. We were absolutely shocked to see the hatred and venom being spewed from the mouths of those who opposed a group of children praying for 10-15 minutes on Friday afternoons. I could no longer stand idle. A Facebook event was created to raise awareness about the issue. My friend, who was also the organizer, added me to the Facebook page as an admin. Over 200 people clicked "attending" yet no one showed up. The organizer of the event and I prepared posters for the rally. I came prepared with signs that said "Thank you TDSB," and "No to Religious Segregation." There were only a few Muslims. A woman came up to me and said, "Go back home, you don't belong here." I simply responded by saying, "I do belong here, I was born and raised in Canada." She got frustrated and walked away.

Now this is where the excitement began. An Egyptian woman approached me and asked me why I was protesting. I began speaking with her but she started yelling at me, saying I shouldn't be there. She found out I was Arab and started speaking to me in Arabic, reciting verses in the Quran that suited her argument. In hindsight, what she and those who kill in the name of Islam today have in common is that they cherry-pick verses, pulling them out of context, and use them as the basis of their arguments. When she started the commotion, a crowd started to form around me and the next thing I knew, there were news reporters around and cameras were pointing at us. Some twenty people surrounded me, yelling things such as: "Islam is a satanic cult!" "Where is your hijab?" and "Why are you wearing pants?"

The most intriguing part about the opposition was that there were groups from other faiths, Hindu, Christian, and Jewish, who obviously demonstrated their Islamophobia, holding up signs saying, "Stop Islamic Infiltration in Public Schools," and "Today Muslims Want Prayers in Schools, Tomorrow What Will They Ask For?" All this about children using an unused cafeteria to pray for 10-15 minutes on Friday afternoons.

I was asked by a number of reporters to speak more about the issue. Many articles were published, a video recording of the

Egyptian woman yelling at me was put up on YouTube, and all of a sudden, the community had awoken. I told the reporters how important it is for young students to practice their faith in a manner that does not impose or force their beliefs on others. A few days later the video went viral. The title of the video was "Brave Muslim Girl at TDSB Friday Protest," uploaded by a community member, who later became a friend and great supporter of the cause. I went home that day feeling proud for having stood up for those who were unable to stand up for themselves.

A friend of mine found and watched the video and asked me "Can I post it on your Facebook wall?" At first I did not want anyone to watch it, but more people became aware of its existence. I received many messages from people in the Muslim community thanking me for doing this. I received other messages from the opposing side trying to convince me to leave my "Islamic beliefs" and to convert to their faith. I want to be clear, those who were in opposition are not representative of other faiths. Just as the media likes to show the most extreme examples of Islam, these groups represent extreme versions of their respective faiths. I had many Christian, Jewish, and Hindu supporters, and supporters from other backgrounds as well.

I met with many individuals who supported the cause and members of the Valley Park community who wanted to ensure that prayers stayed in schools. It was made clear that the prayer accommodation was for everyone, not only for Muslim students. Had the Christian or Jewish prayers, which happen to fall on Sunday and Saturday respectively, fallen on a weekday, the school would have accommodated such prayers. We did find out, however, that there was Jewish accommodation made at a particular TDSB public school. During Jewish holidays, the cafeteria at that school would be closed and students would have to eat elsewhere. The community and Jewish students used the cafeteria to offer prayers.

Once it was official that the prayers would remain, we hosted a TDSB Appreciation Day in front of the TDSB headquarters on

September 18, 2011. We invited the students of Valley Park Middle School, and teachers, trustees, and students from universities and other TDSB public schools. A counter protest by our rivals was expected. The police was notified of our event and put up a barrier between us in order to maintain the safety of the children. Together we made a final statement thanking the TDSB for making the right decision. We sang the Canadian national anthem and those who care about human rights went home happy.

I was featured in a documentary called *The Muslim Toronto*, directed by Salmaan Al Farsi. I spoke about my experience during this time and the importance of thanking the TDSB for allowing prayers in schools. In my third year of university, I became more involved at the York campus. I ran in the election for the Director of the York Federation of Students Union and won the position.

In my fourth year at York, during the 2013-2014 term, I was the president of the Middle Eastern Students' Association. Surprisingly, even in Canada, men continue to want to diminish the role of women. When I decided to run for president, my political and religious views were challenged. Because I am a woman, because I am of Syrian descent and did not agree with certain political views, and because I come from a Muslim Sunni family, there were "problems" with my identity. The president at the time did not think I was a suitable individual to run for the position despite being a founder and a strong contributor to the maintenance of the organization.

As I get older, many of my friends and family members are beginning to enter the married state. I began to explore my spirituality. Starting in 2011, every Friday I have written Friday "statuses." I write stories, poems, and quote religious texts and authors in order to inspire and provide some sort of guidance to those who are interested. When I read other statuses on Facebook and twitter, they were inspirational and helped me become more motivated to do good in the world. That's what inspired me to do the same. Why not highlight an important day in Islam and inspire everyone, not just Muslims. I wanted to spread the message of love, peace and passion. I helped myself by helping others.

I support those who wear the hijab and I support those who don't wear the hijab. Hijab is a choice. Often difficult, but the choice has to be made by the woman. If a woman chooses to wear it, it is not for the sake of anyone else but for herself and God. Neither her mother nor her father can order her to wear it. Neither her brother nor her husband can order her to wear it. It is a choice and as such should be respected. By the same token, women who decide that the hijab is not for them should be respected equally and should not be ridiculed or disrespected.

I've always had an inclination towards wearing the hijab, but I am also a strong believer that modesty and respect can be shown without wearing the hijab. I have received many private messages from Muslim women showing gratitude for representing Islam in such a respectable manner. I feel I have a duty to represent women of Islam that do not wear the hijab. When I have conversations with others, and they ask if I am Muslim, I can see how they look at me. A different perspective is seen when you are not immediately judged by what you are wearing. You can teach others the way of Islam with your attitude, humility, and grace. The point of Islam is to teach others what we are taught by God and our prophets (peace be upon them). Let's teach others that just by smiling, you are giving charity.

No Suitable Boy

ASHI MUNIR

MY PARENTS CAME to Canada in the mid-1970s from Karachi. I was born and raised here. I lived quite a sheltered life, always cheerful, optimistic, and treating life as one big adventure with love in my heart for everyone around me. Mom had me young—at seventeen; she had married and come to Canada at sixteen years of age. Dad is a decade older. I am the eldest grandkid on my mom's side of the family and also the eldest on my dad's side who reside in Canada. I have three younger siblings. My sister married a couple of years ago, and I now have a smart adorable little niece; my youngest brother recently married.

Although my parents were pretty sociable, I didn't have any brown friends of my age group who I could share things with. I had a lot of faith in God, but I did not wear the hijab or pray five times a day. Back then we didn't even have as many halal meat stores as we do now. Dad would go to Kensington Market's Jewish district and zabiha the chickens. We would say Bismillah and eat at restaurants (no pork of course). Now, with halal options available everywhere, we avoid non-halal food. I made my first real brown friends in Grade 11, but even then there was a bit of a distance, as they were both from Pakistan and, well, I wasn't as fluent in Urdu as I am now.

Who doesn't dream of wanting someone to call their own? At twenty-one, you've got romantic ideals and notions of true love from watching romantic movies. You dream about Mr Right. That was the same time when Mom decided I should get married, although I hadn't even graduated yet. She felt education wasn't as important and I could always resume studies after marriage. Back then the majority of the Pakistani families we knew were all finding brides from back home, to bring more family here in Canada. Most of the time I was overlooked because I didn't fit the traditional mold. I wasn't thin, fair-skinned or with straight silky hair; I was of average size, average skin tone, and had curly unmanageable hair. Sometimes I was even taller than the guy. The Pakistani guys older than me also had a different mind-set.

The Son of the Penthouse Owner

That summer, my mom had gone on a trip to Pakistan and sent me photos of a guy she thought would be great for me. His family was well-off, they lived in a penthouse in an apartment complex built by an uncle's company, and there was no mother-in-law in the picture. I saw the pictures, wasn't necessarily impressed but I booked a trip to Pakistan. It was more an excuse to visit my extended family than to see the guy, but I thought "what the heck, why not?"

The only problem was he was so dark that, as he sat under the tubelight in the living room, all I could see were his eyeballs. He wore the drabbest attire. A plain white shirt and brown pants. Nothing impressive, but I thought he would chat with me. He didn't speak one word to me; he didn't speak at all. Call me crazy, but aren't these meetings for the guy and girl to get to know each other even in front of chaperones? His father was doing all the talking and seemed more social. This really upset me. Which century were we living in? My father had spent money on a plane ticket so that I would go and see him and there was no effort on this guy's part. Next day, I found myself with my mom and maternal grandfather.

Trying to make them see my point of view was hard, but they gave in reluctantly. After that was over, some of my aunts and uncles told me they were glad I had said no, after initially taking my mom's side because they were scared of her.

The Green-Card Holder

On that same trip, I met a lady at my grandparents' home who came to see me; her son was in the US. But seeing that I had tanned, having gone shopping in the afternoons in preparation of my uncle's wedding, she seemed a bit disappointed. Her son wanted someone who looked like the girls in the US. That very evening, one of my mom's cousins came over and that aunty immediately showed interest in her for her son. My mom's cousin had flawless porcelain skin and brown hair. Aunty left our home disappointed, since the cousin, though young, was already married with two little kids.

The Politician's Son

When Mom's youngest sister and her family came to settle in Canada, I was elated. I was very close to my mom's side of the family, and my aunt and I had shared a room once when we lived with my grandfather in Dubai for a brief period. When she came to Canada, my aunt found an affordable apartment close to our home and became friends with one couple. When the man's nephew came for a visit, my aunt found out he was the son of an ex-minister of Pakistan. I was introduced to him. He was two years younger than me, but about the same height. Neither of us talked much. I didn't care for that. Within two weeks I was told that I was marrying him. Calls came in from UK regarding the wedding. I was in total confusion since I must have spoken to him for a total of ten minutes. Things were going way too fast around me to make sense. Even my parents knew each other for six years before they got married.

Then I met the neighbours and their daughter goes, "You and my uncle are getting married!" Everyone seemed happy around me. I wasn't raised this way, I wasn't submissive, and neither were my folks. I wasn't going to just accept what they wanted for me. I managed to get the guy's address in UK from my aunt and posted him two letters (just in case one got lost in the mail) asking him what made him think that I was going to marry him when we only met for ten minutes. I didn't hear from him or his family again.

Microsoft Certified Expert/Model

My mom's best friend from high school had a nephew in Pakistan she wanted to set me up with. He was doing his Microsoft certification at that time, which was a big thing back then (now even a child knows MS Office products). He was also into modeling. One of my mom's brothers went to see him and the guy served tea. He was upfront and honest about wanting to move to the US or Canada. We got a couple of his modeling pictures. He was actually around the same age group as I was so I mailed him a card just to say hello. To my surprise, a few weeks later I receive a card from him in the mail. I took it as a positive sign and then asked for his email address and sent him an email. No reply for a couple of months, so I asked his cousin (my mom's best friend's daughter) about him. I found out that he had broken up with his fiancée and was finding ways to get back at her, and that's how I came into the picture. I forgot all about him. Six months later, my mom, sis, and I were heading out to a wedding show in Mississauga just for the ambiance and to check out the latest trends. We were almost out the door when the doorbell rang. The model's older brother had come to see me at the request of his mother. We took this in stride, entertained them for a bit, answered questions. I noticed that the older brother's friend, who had come along, had long pointy nails on his baby fingers. I figured it must be because he snorted drugs. After they left, we went on our merry way to the wedding show and never heard from that family again.

The Surgeon-in-Training

A few years later, after I had suffered a major heartbreak from a guy I had met in university, my mom took it as an opportunity to set me up with a distant cousin of hers. Mom belittled the guy who broke my heart, but I accepted the idea of this new "rishta." From what we were told, he was on a scholarship at a university in the UK. He was in the US for a bit and my dad drove me to Detroit to meet him. We had dinner. He told me he was studying to become a surgeon and joked about how his credit cards were all maxed out. I thought, ok, he seems nice enough, maybe I will grow to like him over time. He also complained about how his brother was totally into his wife, so much so that he forgot his own family.

After our meeting in Detroit, we spoke over the phone a couple of times. I felt like I was avoiding his calls more than trying to get to know him. I even got to meet his brother, his wife, and her family. They were a loving couple and the guy was hardly the negative picture that his brother had portrayed. He seemed more responsible and I remember wishing I had met him instead. The surgeon-in-training spoke a mile a minute and seemed a little too cocky. I wasn't into him and my mom knew it.

One night, Mom comes into my room and tells me that I am no princess, that I am not beautiful (leave it to your parent for putting you down), and that she will not have me marrying outside of my culture or religion. She then proceeded to ask me why I didn't want to marry the guy. She had me standing in my room in silence for a whole twenty minutes before I got the courage to share my doubts. I ended up packing a suitcase and taking a train. I hadn't thought of a destination yet, when I got a call from the guy's aunt and ended up spending two days at her daughter's place before my dad came to pick me. I was also given a promise ring. I never cared enough to wear it, because the sentiments weren't there. Everyone was happy around me, I wasn't. I felt nothing. It was a decision I was accepting for others.

A month later, I got a phone call from the surgeon-in-training. He told me that he knew from his aunt that I was totally in love with him and that he wanted to marry me in two weeks. You can imagine my surprise. I asked him if he was feeling all right. We barely knew each other. After a bit of prodding, he told me that he had received a letter from his university in UK that since he hadn't shown up for a semester, his student status had been withdrawn. That would affect his student visa. He wanted to move to the US and since Canada was the next best thing, he wanted to get married right away in a mosque and take lots of pictures to show as proof to the immigration officers, since he was living illegally in the States.

That's when I lost my cool. I told him he was crazy to think that I would ever be in love with him, and that he could forget about marrying me. He said he never had anyone yell at him like this before. He would call my father and tell him that if I didn't marry him in two weeks, he would marry someone else. That same evening, Dad told me that the guy had called him and threatened to marry someone else if I didn't do nikah with him in two weeks. Dad calmly told him "By all means, go ahead and marry someone else." He then simply hung up the phone. Mom wasn't too pleased, but I never heard his name again.

A few months later another of Mom's cousins revealed to me that a distant cousin/surgeon-in-training had been in a live-in relationship with a Russian woman for three years, but his mom was not accepting her into the family and was pushing him to marry me. For some reason, it put a smile on my face knowing Mom's epitome of cultural perfection wasn't such a good boy after all.

The HR Consultant

At a wedding, I asked an old friend from high school if he had any friends whom he could set me up with—someone who was born in Canada like us. He did, and it was a friend who was an HR consultant and present at that same wedding. Unfortunately, my friend's mother had the same idea, and was trying to get me to set me up with the HR guy as well. Talk about awkward. The day I was supposed to meet the guy for coffee, my friend's mom called to tell my own mom about it, and the next thing you know I am being yelled at to be on my best behaviour, and that I was not getting any younger. Leave it to her to make me feel low and insignificant. We argued and I left the house angry and upset.

I realize they have good intentions, but parents need to know when to back off. The whole time I was with the HR guy, he tried his best to be funny and charming, but that irritated me more and made me want to tell him off. He was two years older than me, but spoke a Pakistani dialect I had never heard of until then. When I found out that he had left Canada as a kid and came back when he was older, I was dismayed. He was more Pakistani than Canadian.

He even knew how to read and write Urdu, knew about Pakistan's history, geography, and politics while I did not. He had a different cultural upbringing and we weren't right for each other. I ended up being up front with him about the argument that occurred with my mom earlier. I agreed with him that he was not at fault. We parted amicably. I kept flip-flopping about him afterwards but just couldn't see a future with him. In our last phone conversation, I apologized to him for my behaviour, but then told him that we could only be friends. I gave him the name of a friend who I thought would be more suited for him. However, things didn't work out with them either.

I am a very social person, don't get me wrong. I just haven't had luck with Pakistani men, and it is not like I haven't made the effort. There is more of a desi population now than there was two decades ago, so girls now won't have to deal with all the mess that the generation before them has had to deal with. There are more desi kids raised in Canada now. Parents don't need to look in the homelands for suitable mates for their children and in the process make their kids' lives hell. More kids are finding their better halves through friends, colleagues, school, etc. so in a way making things easier for the parent. Daughters should be allowed to pursue their education before marriage and if kids want to marry outside of their own culture or religion, let them learn from their own mistakes. No arranged or immigration sham marriages; no starter marriages and divorces. In my thirties, having lost faith and being plagued by self-doubt thanks to those close to me, if it hadn't been for the intervention of dear friends, I wouldn't have changed my thinking, attitude, and career direction (from financial services to health information management), and moved to a new city in pursuit of further education. I am now working in a hospital in the arctic where there is twenty-four hours of daylight in the summer months, and you can see the northern lights clearly in the winter. I am now open to meeting someone from another culture or faith.

I lost my faith due to "decent religious men" who turned out to be cowardly and immature. I am sorry I was raised in Canada, and not in some place like Karachi, Islamabad, Jeddah, Qatar or Dubai, as that automatically disqualified me from being a potential, even in situations where I actually liked the guy. Call me atheistic if you will. Life treats us all differently and we handle each situation in our own way. I have joined a woman's group online that a friend started. We help each other with fitness trends and life advice. It has grounded me and made me stronger as a person having their support in my life, and I hope that I have returned the favour and made a difference in their lives as well.

Recently my mom reiterated that same old "what will people say" speech but with a new twist. She said that if I don't get married after my youngest brother's wedding, she would make sure that none of my siblings or other relatives would ever speak to me again. Years ago, her words would sting and I would find myself crying in my room and wallowing in self-pity. Now I am stronger. I am wiser. I know she wants the best for me and to see me settled, and I am sure the right man will come along who won't disappear on me the moment things get tough. Until then I have a life to live and lessons to learn. Some people are just meant to find their other half later in life. That is no crime, and it certainly shouldn't be treated as such by any culture. They say everything happens for a reason. I strongly believe in that now.

Love for All, Hatred for None

SADIA KHAN

B Y THE GRACE of God I was born in an Ahmadi Muslim family in Pakistan.

It was a pleasant day when I landed in Toronto with my husband in October 1994. On my way from the airport, I was surprised to see how different it was, compared to how it looked in pictures and how similar it was to Islamabad, in terms of roads, trees and houses. I liked the beautiful fall scenery, trees were changing colours and it was my first time seeing this. A few days later, when I went downtown with my husband then the city appeared somewhat similar to what I saw in pictures; I was amazed to see that the roads were not very wide, and the traffic was congested.

My husband used to live with his friend in Scarborough in a building where 20-25 other Ahmadi Muslim families were also residing. We rented an apartment in the same building and lived there for about nine years. At first, I didn't feel like eating anything because everything tasted different, even water. Later on I realized that I was pregnant.

Shortly after arriving in Canada, I went to the Ministry of Education to have my Bachelor of education degree evaluated and I received a "Letter of Eligibility" for teaching in Ontario. I didn't apply for any jobs, because I was not fluent in speaking English, so

I decided to attend ESL classes first.

But I was ambitious and thought of proceeding for further studies here in Canada. I applied at different universities for doing a masters in chemistry again. I received offers from three universities, but my dream of studying was shattered when I became a mother of a baby girl. I missed my family and especially my mother. With no experience in taking care of a baby, it was the hardest job for me ever, plus doing all the house chores. My husband took three weeks off from work and when he started working again he told me to just make bread for myself and leave everything else for him to do upon his return. He is a very good cook but cooks only occasionally.

One of my very good friends was an Ahmadi Pakistani doctor and she helped me a lot during that time. She used to call me every day to find out if I needed anything or had problems. My husband's cousins and other friends residing in my building also helped me whenever I needed help. For two years I was so busy in taking care of the baby that I couldn't even think of studying or doing any job. But I learned typing and a little bit of word processing from books. When my daughter was two and a half years old, I found a good babysitter and therefore decided to go to the Scarborough Center for Alternative Studies to improve my word processing skills. I also took a course in speaking English effectively. Luckily in 1998 I got on the supply list for teaching in both elementary and secondary schools. Some people think that it is hard to teach high school students, but for me it is easier, especially grades eleven and twelve, as they are more serious in studies and more concerned about getting good marks. I did many teaching assignments during this time but couldn't get a regular job. They used to say that I didn't have enough experience, now they say they prefer fresh graduates.

At the beginning, I used to wear just pants, coat and shirt, but no scarf or hijab, because I thought it would look awkward; there were very few Muslim teachers at the time and I didn't see anyone wearing hijab. I also thought that the students might make fun of me, and the other teachers would not be able to communicate with me freely. There was one more reason. We had to shake hands with the interviewers, and I felt that it would make us both uncomfortable. Islam does not allow shaking hands with men, but I had no choice.

Covering ourselves is mandatory in Islam, and it seems in other religions too. During the time when I didn't cover my head at my job, I always felt that I was not covered properly or completely. I also thought that if I did not wear the hijab, I couldn't expect my daughters to wear it. And so I started wearing a scarf two years ago.

I used to think carefully before speaking, to avoid any mistake and provide the students a chance to make fun of me; now I am not so worried.

The motto of our Ahmadiyya Muslim Organization is "Love for All and Hatred for None," and that is my motto too. The Organization was founded in 1889 by Hazrat Mirza Ghulam Ahmad of Qadian, India who said that he was told by God that he was Imam Mahdi and the promised Messiah. Many Muslims accepted him and found him to be righteous in his claim; my grandparents were among those. My maternal grandfather was a medical doctor and my paternal grandfather was the headmaster of a school. Other Muslims do not consider Ahmadi Muslims as Muslims and still wait for the Messiah.

Following a bloody campaign against Ahmadi Muslims by mullahs in Pakistan, in 1974 the Government announced under their pressure that Ahmadis are not Muslims. I was very young at that time, but I remember people throwing stones at our house and writing abuses on the door and walls of our house. To save our lives we had to take refuge in Rabwah, Pakistan at our grandparents' house for three months. To this day Ahmadi Muslims are subjected to persecution and imprisonment for practicing Islam, and many have been brutally murdered. Ahmadis cannot recite the Holy Quran in front of others or write or say the kalima, which is the declaration of the Muslim faith. Some Ahmadi Muslims are even charged for simply saying "Assalam-o-alaikum" meaning, "peace be on you." It seems as if the Pakistani government, instead of condemning these mullahs, is backing them. Ahmadi Muslims are also suffering in other parts of the world, like Bangladesh and Indonesia.

Many Ahmadi Muslims have taken refuge in other countries, such as UK, Germany, and Canada. Our present Khalifa resides in London, UK. My husband came to Canada in 1989 as a refugee after his uncle was martyred because of his faith. Last year one of his nephews, a heart specialist in the United States, went to volunteer at a hospital in Pakistan; he was martyred shortly after his arrival in front of his wife and three-year-old son. And a few years ago, suicide bombers attacked one of our mosques in Lahore. More than eighty people were killed.

When I came to Canada, I went to the annual convention of our organization in Maple, Ontario, and was surprised to see such a large number of Ahmadi Muslims gathered in Canada. In Pakistan there is a ban on us for meeting in large gatherings. Our organization is growing in numbers. Our website is www.alislam.org and we have also launched a satellite TV channel "MTA" that can be watched anywhere in the world. We are now able to watch live Friday sermons of our Khalifa and other events happening live across the globe. Our organization is the most peaceful of all organizations. In our view, the only jihad that is acceptable nowadays is the jihad of the pen. By writing we can win the hearts of millions.

I served as the General Secretary of the Ahmadiyya women's organization in Scarborough for about six years, and then I served as a General Secretary for the Durham jamat. I also volunteered for the Ahmadiyya Sunday School as a teacher. Now my elder daughter is a teacher's assistant.

When my children were young, I was worried about the negative influence of the larger society on them and I wanted them to know the true teachings of Islam, so they could make their own decisions. Some of the bad influences that I am talking about are, first, the dresses that do not cover the body properly, and second, the relationship between boys and girls outside of marriage, and third, drinking, and fourth, gambling. These are prohibited in Islam.

Before marriage I was passionate about working, but I realized that it is hard for a woman to do well at her job while taking good care of the kids. I realized why Islam asked men to work to earn money to fulfill all the needs of the family and asked women to stay at home to take care of the family. My kids are a bit older now and have started helping around the house.

For some time after getting a driving license I didn't drive, as my husband used to pick me up and drop me off at the school, so for the first two years I didn't even know the location of the schools. But when my husband got a job in Chicago after the completion of his computer networking course, I lived for about three months without his help. During that time I learned a lot of things. I drove everywhere and did all the shopping. Still, it was a difficult period. I remember one day my son had fever and I had no medicine at home; I couldn't leave the kids alone at home, so I took them with me to get the medicines.

In 2003 we decided to buy a house instead of renting. We found our dream house in Pickering that was close to all amenities and not far from my job either. After we moved, I started working with the Durham District School Board also. My experiences have not been pleasant though, and so I still prefer going to Toronto for most of my supply teaching work. I also like teaching in Scarborough, I like their diversity and multicultural environment. Mostly, I get calls from the TDSB. I make many new friends from different parts of the world doing supply teaching.

After my father's demise and my brother's immigration to England with his family, my mother was left alone in the house in Pakistan, and so we invited her to live with us in Canada. She arrived in 2005. She took good care of my kids too and taught them the Holy Quran, Urdu, and math. Now she lives independently in a seniors home in Ajax. My sister came to live in Canada too, since her family's life was in danger in Pakistan. One of my cousins is expected to arrive soon, having received death threats. We pray constantly for the safety of our other family members and our friends.

I am a Canadian now and I love this country as I love Pakistan. I thank Allah that I live in the best country in the world, where the health and education system are good and the people are nicer and friendlier. They are more welcoming towards people of other countries, compared to Europe and America. They have many good qualities that are prescribed in the Holy Quran and by our beloved Prophet Muhammad (peace be upon him). May God bless all of us and show all of us the right path, Ameen.

Letters to Rumi

MEHAROONA GHANI

RECYCLED PAGES

Do you know what you are?
You are a manuscript of a divine letter.
You are a mirror reflecting a noble face.
This universe is not outside of you.
Look inside yourself;
everything that you want,
you are already that – Rumi[1]

Dear Rumi,

What if you were caught in a hairball?

I awoke to limp fingers—my arm was pinned in an awkward position. I shot up in bed, shook my arm—waited. Is this what paralysis felt like? The fingers became conscious. Then, I continued my morning gratitude practice:

vision – checked;

      hearing – checked;

           appendages – checked;

                speech – checked;

                    memory – checked.

I was thirty-four when I was told I had MS. That's all I needed: another barrier. I was eight-years-old when I learned I was different in Golden, British Columbia. Yup, those white kids surrounded my sister and I, made fun of our names and yelled "Paki" and "Hindu." We broke free, ran home and asked our parents about the words.

Now in my forties I still don't quite belong. This Rocky Mountain born and raised Golden girl who had labels imposed on her, or who had chosen labels and tossed them out, is unraveling that hairball.

Rumi —

you. Embody.

My. Every experience,

every one. My. Skin. Hair.

Veins. Bones. Soul. Senses.

Swallowed. You. Spit out.

Hairball. I. Unravel. A

WTF attitude. I.

Write. Letters

to you.

Love always,
Meharoona (your light of the moon)

Limitations

> *Study me as much as you like, you will not know me,*
> *for I differ in a hundred ways from what you see me to be.*
> *Put yourself behind my eyes and see me as I see myself,*
> *for I have chosen to dwell in a place you cannot see*
> *— Rumi[2]*

Dear Rumi,

"What kind of Muslim are you: Sunni, Shia, Ismaili? No Sunni would write this."

"Your poetry is exotic."

"This is a lesbian poem. You can't be straight."

"I know exactly what this is about—your pussy!"

"You better be careful, you might get a fatwa on your head!"

"How can a virgin write this way? How can you be sensual?"

I received this feedback during readings in British Columbia— from people of colour, white people, straight, gay, lesbian, queer, feminists, academics, construction workers, people born in Canada, immigrants, Muslims, non-Muslims, all genders. Why does society obsess with where I fit?

My seeds blossomed to reveal calligraphy on each petal . . . I continue to be studied . . .

Open your arms,
let me spread –
over – your chest.
Hold your pulse
against breasts.
Brush fingers
along the hair on your head.
Lips near nape.
We crave –
connection.
It was through our eyes,
we saw the other,
heard beats,
exhaled,
concealed,
pushed and pulled

at unseen places . . .

Love always,
Meharoona (your light of the moon)

The Cost of Choice

> *"The world's flattery and hypocrisy is a sweet morsel:*
> *eat less of it, for it is full of fire.*
> *Its fire is hidden while its taste is manifest,*
> *but its smoke becomes visible in the end."* – Rumi[3]

Dear Rumi,

2002—I agreed to mentor Muslim girl participants at a girls' conference about race and identities. I peered at their perm-like hair, straight hair, short hair, dark and light hair, dark and light skin. Some of them wore low-riser jeans with tight t-shirts while others wore less revealing pants and loose tops. They all could have passed off as any young girl.

The girls stared with expressions of curiosity. Each introduced herself: ages ranged from fourteen to sixteen, from different ethnic and cultural backgrounds mostly of Middle Eastern, Asian and African heritages and from various schools in BC.

By the second day during lunch we met at the Women's Centre and the girls opened up. "What do you think about showing skin?" asked the girl whose fashionable tribal hoop earrings jingled while she pulled at bits of curly hair away from the bells.

"Showing skin . . . in what way?" I asked.

"You know—like wearing sleeveless tops, skirts, or shorts. That stuff."

Oh Miss Earrings, how shall I answer when I'm conflicted?

"Why?" I asked.

"Muslim women can't really show skin. It's in the Quran," said the girl pulling at purple string embroidered onto the hem of her long-sleeved top.

"Yeah, we can't . . . " began Miss Earrings. "When I leave home I wear a hijab, baggy clothes and no makeup. That's what my dad wants. But, once at school I change clothes and put on makeup. This is me." She pointed to her tube top that bared her soft belly and her low riser pants that revealed a hint of a thong. "If my dad saw this, he'd lose it."

I'd lose it too. "Did something happen to you?" I held back my own prude-like revulsion of this 'sexploitation' of thongs poking out from jeans.

"Yeah! Since 9/11, I've had guys try to pull my hijab off or students make fun of me. I don't want them to know I'm Muslim anymore," said Miss Earrings.

My eyes widened. *Those racist A-holes!*

"Me too. But, I don't wear clothes like her," said Embroidery Girl pointing at Miss Earrings.

"Hey, I like these clothes. Guys look at me. I feel beautiful. Men ask me if I want a ride."

Holy! They're asking you because you look like a hooker! Wait! I'm terrible, I can't believe I just thought that! I'm pro-sexual identity if the woman is in control and has choice, but at fourteen what does a girl know?

"What do you do?" My fingers folded tightly together. *Those pricks!*

"I say no. But, I like their attention."

Thank God you said no! You are beautiful. Give it time. I stared at Miss Earrings who looked eighteen with her well-endowed breasts under her white tube top, her blue eye shadow emphasized her Cleopatra eyes and her dark pink lipstick accentuated her mouth. I pictured her as my daughter. I worried. "Are you trying to fit in?" I felt sadness and love.

"Yeah, that and also I don't like it when my dad forces me to cover up." She pointed to Embroidery Girl's loose ensemble.

"I see . . . " I glanced at her clothes too thinking about my own kind of conservative, yet sexy look. The girls eagerly waited for an answer within the safe woman's space. "I don't have a problem with showing skin . . . but, for me, it does depend on how much."

God, we live in a hypocritical patriarchal world.

"Look, we live in a world where some think women showing a lot of skin are loose or 'asking for it', sometimes there can be violence . . ."

"But then when were you allowed to do what you wanted?"

"In small spurts . . . not until I was older. I wasn't even allowed to go to a dance until grade 12 . . . when I graduated!"

"Really?" The girls laughed.

"I was thirteen when I could put nail polish on or wear high heels . . . AND this was only after my mom saw photos of her fashionable nieces in Kenya."

My sister and I argued with Mom, 'see they're doing it, why can't we?'

The girls relaxed on the couch. So did I. "Maybe when you're sixteen your dad will let you do certain things."

"Don't they trust me?" asked Miss Earrings.

"My parents always said: 'we trust you, it's other people we don't trust.' Perhaps this is what your dad is thinking too." I moved from the couch to sit cross-legged on the ground. The girls followed and we sat in a closer round. "Do you think showing your skin makes you more beautiful or empowered?" I asked Miss Earrings.

"Yeah. All the girls do it."

"Why?"

"Because boys like it." Miss Earrings readjusted her tube top to push her breasts up and pulled her low-riser jeans up at the back to cover the tip of her thong. "What do you think?"

Christina Aguilera's "Dirrty" video suddenly popped in my head in her next to nothing attire, gyrating hips in a wrestling rink while pumped up half naked men cheered her on. *It's total exploitation! Heck, if Christina is going to be suggestive in stringy underwear, why not just bare it all?*

"So . . . is it really for you or for the boys?" Air particles bounced while the sunlight moved across the room.

"We're told we have to dress a certain way because the religion tells us to and if we don't we're sinners," said one of the quiet girls whose freckles quivered on the tip of her nose when she spoke.

"Actually there's a lot of misinformation out there." *It's an uphill patriarchal battle.* I refrained from sharing Muslim feminists scholarly analysis.

"Didn't your parents tell you it's a sin to show skin?" asked Miss Earrings.

"No. They were just worried about some guy attacking me. Actually, when I was twelve my dad agreed that I could take Kung Fu lessons. 'So you know how to fight off any asshole,' was what my dad said."

Laughter erupted. "Cool," said Freckles.

"Well . . . they were like any other parents: worried about daughters. I wasn't allowed to date or go out after 9 PM or go to parties or dances where there was alcohol or sleepover at white people's homes. My parents thought that I'd be corrupted." The International Women's Day poster of the women of colour stared down at our circle, with their flexed biceps and the slogan "We Can Do It!" floating above their heads.

"I've learned it's not right to assume that other people might not be good because they are different, but I'm also kind of glad my parents looked out for me." I tapped Miss Earrings on the hand. "What does your mom think?"

"She agrees with my dad."

"I have to be honest I don't like the fact that these men you don't know are offering rides. I can understand your parents' worry." I breathed in, "these guys . . . they only see your boobs." The girls snickered at "boob."

"Well, if you got it, flaunt it," said Miss Earrings.

"Okay . . . so . . . do you know what to do if he grabs your boobs? Sorry to be blunt."

"Fight with my nails?" Embroidery Girl clawed the air.

"Yes! Anyway you can . . . " I held Embroidery Girl's hands and looked back at Miss Earrings. "What if you had a daughter and someone grabbed her?"

"I'd let her wear what ever she wanted." I looked to the ground while mixed feelings tugged at freedom to choose versus living in a patriarchal sexist society. I released triggers of feminist theory.

"I agree. No one should be forced to do something they don't want to. But truly, how would you react?"

"Well . . . I'd be worried too."

"Try talking to your parents."

"I don't think they'll understand."

I don't know. I get you. I get your parents. I get it: mixed feelings, rebellious, the struggle between what's really choice or what's shaped by society.

Rumi, perhaps there is something to be said to cover women up,
    but is it at the cost of taking choice away?

What is it about women's skin — the sweetest landscape —
that sends man into vengeful missions to claim a plot on our
    bodies?
I'm unable to remove the image
of India's daughter
brutally torn apart in 2012
with her intestines
pulled out. Left to die.
She was blamed for being out late at night
with an unrelated man (He was a friend.
Beaten unconscious).
Her lesson — gang rape.

Like animals on a hunt . . .
mouths wide-opened
sucking on the world's
flattery and hypocrisy of

the skin's canvas
owned by a woman.

Piece by piece,
plot by plot,
landscape sold, packaged
to the highest bidder –
morsels swallowed . . . [4]
Tell me Rumi, when does the smoke become visible?

Love always,
Meharoona (your light of the moon)

Manufacturing Islam

You think of yourself as a citizen of the universe.
You think you belong to this world of dust and matter.
Out of this dust you have created a personal image,
and have forgotten about the essence of your true origin
– Rumi[5]

Dear Rumi,

While in prayer position, I folded my hands in silence and asked
the Divine what to do during Ramadan since fasting was impossible with my MS. "Wear the hijab for thirty-days and pray five times
per day," came out of my mouth.

I got ready for my weekly walk. Put on my grey sweat-pants, blue
grey t-shirt from Mauritius and Nike runners. The white hijab went
perfect. The bonus—no one knew that under the scarf hid a bad-
hair-day. My friend Hema joined me for a walk in the Shaughnessy
area.

"I see you're wearing your head scarf. It looks great."
"Thanks!"
"Is there a special reason?"

"Ramadan . . . and since I can't fast, I committed to wearing the scarf and praying five times a day." I didn't get into an explanation about the longing I felt to connect to a Divine.

"Good for you."

"Look there's Hycroft. I heard it was haunted."

"Really."

"Yeah. I went on a tour and our guide said there were ghosts . . . " I caught my breath, "hello . . . " We passed a construction worker whose tight white t-shirt outlined his muscular upper arms and chest, revealing a hint of a tattoo below his collarbone. "I've always wanted a tattoo . . . wait . . . I don't think I should be staring at him while I'm wearing a hijab and observing Ramadan!"

"This commitment of yours isn't going to be easy," laughed Hema.

Damn. I mean darn!

"So tell me—are you serious about it?" asked my sister.

"I don't know. My *hijabi* friends have said wearing it is obligatory. I do find it liberating. Men have been treating me differently."

"How?"

"They were more respectful. Offered me seats on buses or opened doors for me."

"Wonder why?"

"No one ever does that when I'm not wearing a scarf."

"Maybe they think you're a subservient woman?"

"I don't know. Could be a power thing? I kind of liked the gentleman behaviour."

Rumi, I concluded that it wasn't the scarf that connected me to a Divine. Somewhere in the re-creation of a personal image I found the origin is within—maybe I'm a lot closer to the Divine than I realized.

Love always,
Meharoona (your light of the moon)

Other Side of Confessions

Seek the wisdom that will untie your knot.
Seek the path that demands your whole being.
Leave that which is not, but appears to be.
Seek that which is, but is not apparent. – Rumi[6]

Dear Rumi,

I recalled the visit of a university professor with a background in the history of Islam, Christianity and gender relations. She joined our Muslim potluck gathering at our university's student lounge. The professor asked us why we thought more Muslim men were marrying non-Muslim women and why more Muslim women were single?

"It's easier to date outside of the faith. Less baggage," said one of the guys who openly dated.

"Yeah, I find dating without all the cultural and religious stuff is just easier," said another guy.

"Well, some Muslim guys date non-Muslim women for only 'one thing', I said while I watched the older aunties and uncles get uncomfortable with the unsaid. I didn't have the courage to say out loud—S E X. I didn't have the courage to reveal that some male Muslim friends told me it was only about sex. I was pissed to learn that when it came time for marriage, some of these guys followed family pressures and their families expected a Muslim woman to be a virgin! Yet—if a Muslim woman dated, her reputation would be ruined therefore she'd be deemed unmarriageable . . . OR . . . in some extreme situations violence.

"Women are damned on all accounts." I locked my arm in my friend's arm to get in line for food.

"I've finally met the right man, Mom. It's like the Prophet Mohamed and Khadija story."

"So, now you're comparing yourself to the Prophet's wife (peace be upon her)?" said Mom. "You might not want to give this as an example to your Mr Right. It will freak him out." This came from a woman whose marriage was arranged and who had been with only one man for over forty years.

"No, not comparing. Yeah, no way I'm gonna say this to him! I only wanted to verify in the Quran that being with a man ten years younger than me . . . is . . . well . . . actually normal in the eyes of the Divine."

"You're normal," said Mom.

I had never dated. Prospective marriage suitors were seen in large groups. My first heartbreak was at twenty-three—he fit the bill—Muslim, South Asian, raised and educated in Canada. After three years of group encounters, I wrote him a poem and gave it to him one spring day; then I got a blow.

"You're pretty, but I want someone with fair skin, and you know . . . green eyes and well . . . long blonde hair."

"You've just described a white woman. What are you doing with me?"

No answer.

Forward many years later, I'm no longer looking for that virgin-Muslim-South-Asian-man. He doesn't exist. Not only was Mr Right white, he was a non-Muslim, an ex-Mormon, respected my choice of not drinking alcohol, not eating pork and not having sex before marriage, and he was ten years younger—more Muslim than any Muslim man I had ever met. I'm in my forties learning to date and communicate the sacredness of intimacy.

Rumi, sometimes life is like a game of snakes and ladders. Roll the dice and move up ladders or down snakes. There's no right or wrong path. It's a game of chance.

I tipped over confessions –
cheeks flushed knitted feelings.
Noble threads undone.
Relished calm body,
breathing moments.[7]

My nose pressed
under left ear
near jaw line . . .
"I fit right here with you."

Love always,
Meharoona (your light of the moon)

The above is an excerpt from a longer work, "Letters to Rumi."

Notes

1 Shahram T Shiva, *Hush, Don't Say Anything to God: Passionate Poems of Rumi*, (Jain Publishing Company, 1991).

2 John Baldock, *The Essence of Rumi*, 2005, http//craigconsidinetcd.word-press.com/2012/06/25/rumis-inspiration/ in Divan-I Shams-I Tabrizi 1372: A1: 168.

3 http://www.goodreads.com/quotes/tag/rumi

4 Poem inspired by: Udwin, Leslee. (2012) "India's Daughter" *The Passionate Eye*, CBC News Network, 21 June.

5 *Hush, Don't Say Anything to God: Passionate Poems of Rumi*, in http://www.goodreads.com/quotes/tag/rumi

6 Azmina Melita Kolin and Maryam Mafi (translators), *Rumi: Hidden Music*, (Barnes & Noble, 2009 reprint), 68.

7 Slightly altered erasure from Taffy Brodesser-Akner "Quotables" and "Confessions of a Chronic Crier," *Oprah Magazine*, February 2013.

My Journey With the Niqab

ZUNERA ISHAQ

ELEANOR ROOSEVELT ONCE said, "A woman is like a tea bag, you never know how strong she is until she gets into hot water." I am one such woman. Some Canadians will recognize my name from news headlines. I am the Muslim woman whom Prime Minister Stephen Harper would not allow to take the oath of Canadian citizenship because I wear a niqab that covers the lower half of my face. This is my chance to tell you who I am behind the veil.

I am a proud niqab-wearing woman of Pakistani origin. I immigrated to Canada with my husband in 2008. I am a university graduate and the mother of three children. I chose to live in Canada for several reasons. I love the beautiful weather of this country, especially the snow season. And I love this country for its respect for multicultural values which ensure that the individual's freedom to make personal choices related to religion will be safeguarded.

In Pakistan I grew up in a household where education was the main focus. My father was a professor of economics and my four brothers and four sisters have all attended university and earned degrees in marketing, chemistry, journalism and medicine. We chose our fields of study without any pressure or influence from our parents. My father believed in the freedom of opinion and he gave all his children the freedom to make their own choices.

It is worth mentioning here that my father belongs to a landowning family in the Punjab province, where the focus has always been on multiplying land and wealth. He was the only one in his family to go to university, and went on to receive a master's degree. Following his example, his cousin also went to university, becoming an engineer, but none of his children attended university. My father wanted his children to achieve the highest level of education and provided us an environment in which we were encouraged to make our own decisions. My eldest sister was the first girl in our extended family to attend university. She was a brilliant student and earned a graduate degree, and even a certification in homeopathic medicine. In doing all this she sacrificed a marriage prospect because her fiancé said that she was violating tradition by attending a co-ed university and broke off their engagement.

My sister was also the first woman in our family to wear a niqab. Everyone else was completely against this decision, as no female in the family had ever worn a niqab before this. But my father told her that if she really wanted to wear it, he would support her. It was the same when her engagement broke off; he gave her the love and support to stand for what she believed.

I am the youngest child in my family, the "baby" so to speak, and I was given a special "baby" protocol from the very beginning. I realized when I was in grade nine that I could make my own decisions, and I was encouraged at home to voice opinions and make choices. This gave me a lot of confidence and has had an everlasting effect on my personality. I grew up seeing women dependent on the men for almost everything, both inside and outside the house. My own immediate family was an exception; our parents gave us the same freedom of choice as they gave my brothers.

It was in grade eleven that I decided to start covering my face with a niqab. I did this after a detailed study of the Quran and hadith and after carefully considering all the different opinions of scholars within Islam. I found it better for myself to cover my face any time that I went out in public. Two of my sisters wore niqab and the other two sisters chose not to wear it. My family was surprised by my decision. I had always been a tomboy with short hair who used to play with boys of my age, so they were not expecting such a bold decision from me that seemed to be in contrast with my personality.

During my journey with the niqab I went through several phases. After high school I chose a college which was for women only, though it had several men among the support staff. Psychology was one of my majors in college and while doing my lab work I used to cover my face in the presence of male staff. This was not as easy to do as would seem in a country where Islam is the state religion and more than ninety percent of the population is Muslim. The lab assistant was upset but could not say anything to me about it. This did not bother me, but what was frustrating was the attitude of the external examiner of my annual psychology exam. Instead of asking me questions related to the subject, he asked me only about my niqab; he wanted to know the Islamic sources that had led me to wear it, and he ended up mocking me. He took more than forty minutes, and what was more upsetting was that I was the only person left in the room, while my father was waiting anxiously outside.

Some years later I decided to take a master's degree in English literature. Again, everyone at home was surprised by my decision, including my father, who for once joined the others in trying to influence me to change my decision. Their main reason was that I would not fit into the "western" environment of the English literature department. They were right to a large extent and I faced a big challenge during the first few days in my classes, as some of the professors, as well as the head of the department, were secular-minded people who did not like my covered face and mocked me in front of the class. It was even more difficult for me because for the first time I was in a co-ed system. Finally I gathered my nerves and spoke out. I told my teachers that the way I dress was not their business and they must not speak against an individual's choice of dressing.

After that they stopped their comments but they always showed discrimination in marking my term papers and tests. I managed to continue in the department and towards the end of my course it was obvious that many of them had changed their minds about women like me. They no longer assumed that women who covered up their faces had no intelligence or ambition.

During the last semester of my masters program, I got married to a fantastic person who has always helped me to maintain my identity in the way I wish. He has never mocked or discouraged me. We were married in Pakistan, and applied for and got permanent residency in Canada. My husband was a little worried about how I would maintain my niqab in Canada, but he never pressured me about it. He just wondered what would happen if I was ever required to remove it. But all his worries were gone as soon as we landed here in Canada. At the airport when it came time for doing an identity check the officer we were speaking with asked me himself if I would like to show my face to a woman officer. I did not have enough words to thank him; my husband and I were so happy and relieved that God had managed a way for us. I felt as if Allah had chosen us to be in Canada and live with the freedom and respect which was not offered in my own homeland.

I still enjoy this freedom in Canada and I love to work among the wider community. I have contributed in many community projects while wearing my niqab and have raised three children. The projects involve outreach for raising funds for a women's shelter and a local hospital, organizing food drives for community food banks, a Canada Day children's festival, a community information fair, and tree-planting events in the City of Mississauga. For the last two years I have worked with our ward councillor in park-cleaning events, which include Muslim women and children and help to support their integration into the broader Canadian family.

In 2012 I submitted my application to become a citizen. I passed my written test for citizenship in 2013 and a few months later I was called to attend the citizenship ceremony during which I would swear the oath for citizenship. Here I faced a problem, due to the policy introduced two years back by the minister of immigration and citizenship that required me to uncover my face in a roomful of people. This was the first time in Canada when I was being told to uncover myself in a public area with a crowd around me. I was not given a choice; I was told that I had to do this as an obligation. I requested that my oath-taking ceremony be put on hold so that I could find out about my rights and obligations. Unfortunately my request was rejected and the accommodation that I was offered was nothing but ridiculous: I could stand in the very first or very last row during the ceremony but I would still be required to uncover my face.

I got legal help so that I would not have to undergo an unpleasant situation that was contrary to my faith. My lawyer confirmed that the policy was in violation of the Charter of Rights and Freedom, and I decided to challenge the minister's policy in court. This was my own very personal choice. Several of my family members were of the view that I should just go and take the oath, which would be only a matter of a few minutes. But I insisted that if it was my right to practise my faith, then I would do what it took to fight for it. I could not let a policy that violated the rights of a specific group of women go unchallenged. If I did not speak out against it, then how would anyone realize its injustice?

My petition went all the way to the Federal Court of Canada and the outcome was as wonderful as I had prayed for and expected. The Court confirmed that the policy of removing the niqab at the oathing ceremony was against the rights of a specific cultural group and the government had no authority to dictate to any individual what to wear at any time. I felt proud of Canada and was once again very glad that I had chosen to live here. As a niqab-wearing woman I have found more acceptance in Canada than in my country of origin. In Canada we enjoy real democracy and freedom of choice and I am proud of being a part of this great country.

But I was not able to enjoy my victory for long. When I heard

Prime Minister Stephen Harper announce that the government would appeal the court's decision, I was shocked. I did not expect such behaviour from the leader of a free country, especially a country that takes great pride in its multiculturalism. He was refusing to accept the court's decision for his own political ends, to win votes in the upcoming elections.

In November 2015, the new government of Canada, under Justin Trudeau, withdrew the Supreme Court challenge.

There are those who say that if women like me are allowed to wear the niqab then we would soon start to demand for Sharia law as well. This is a silly argument. We are not trying to impose our thoughts or opinions on other people. By asking for the freedom to wear the niqab we are only asking for the right that is given to all the citizens of this multicultural country, where so many people practising different faiths live together in peace and harmony. There is actually no "Sharia Law" in Islam to be implemented here in Canada. The word "sharia" means "law." We already enjoy good and just laws, why would we need any other law?

Embracing Islam in Canada

TAMMARA SOMA

I WAS BORN AND raised partly in Indonesia, in a rapidly urbanizing city called Bogor in West Java. Bogor is humid, rainy, jam-packed with traffic, and home to a million people. I did my last two years of high school in the United States, before moving to Canada to do my undergraduate studies. As a seventeen-year-old living alone in Canada, religion was not my top priority. I was barely a Muslim, barely praying, barely reading the Quran. My goals and my ambitions revolved around academic success: I desired a good career, a good education, and a good relationship, and I wanted to be acknowledged for my hard work.

Education has always been important in my family. Both my parents have doctorates. My father was awarded with a full scholarship to study in Canada, and my mother is a medical doctor who is now a professor in Indonesia. In 2014 I successfully passed my own PhD comprehensive exam; the process had felt like giving birth. But then I literally gave birth to my third child Tierra, a daughter, a mere ten days later. After a two-week "break" I continued my work as a teaching assistant. With my three beautiful and healthy kids, my PhD candidacy almost completed, and my husband supporting pretty much everything I did or ever dreamed of, I understood why some of my colleagues and friends asked me, "How do you do it?"

The grass looked pretty green in my yard. Sheryl Sandberg, the CEO of Facebook has said women should "lean in," and I sure fitted the definition of a woman who leaned in. I worked hard all the way through my pregnancy, and I did not even pause to take a maternity leave. I was juggling multiple projects and commitments. I was leaning in hard, succeeding academically and *seemingly* was happy, yet I was lost inside; something was gnawing at me, I had no peace of mind.

My life was a whirlwind, but the wind became a storm when I received the most horrific phone call. My three-year-old nephew Arfan caught dengue fever back in Indonesia and passed away. It was a cold winter morning, when my mother called me with the news. I felt sick to my stomach. My body became numb. I remember thinking and wishing that I was only dreaming. Please pinch me, please wake me up. I just wanted to sleep and pretend this never happened.

My sister Rathma had also given birth to another baby boy exactly ten days after I gave birth to my daughter Tierra. From Canada to Indonesia, our family was overjoyed with baby bliss. We felt lucky, excited all our kids would play together. Now this. Arfan passed away exactly forty days after his baby brother was born.

Until then I had lived my life as though I were going to live for a hundred years. I took life, health, and my family for granted. My preoccupation was material success, and my happiness was pegged on transient goals. Now for the first time I stared at death squarely in the eyes. The Quran (29:65) says: *And this life of the world is nothing but a pastime and a sport, and the Home of the Hereafter—that indeed is Life, if they but knew!*

I had been spending a lot of time away from my own children, glued to the computer screen, always stressed about impending deadlines, going to conferences. I remember at one point feeling envious of my single friends, who apparently had all the time in the world to sit in coffee shops and write, travel extensively, and read endlessly, books on Foucault, Bourdieu, etc., and analyze Lefebvre at their convenience. I was seeing my family as a burden and my children as a barrier to my becoming a serious academic. Now I never felt happy at leaving my family. Every accomplishment (an award, a publication, a media feature), every "success" caused me anxiety. I would tell my husband: "I can't breathe . . . I can't breathe . . ." My ambitions were like a mirage, I wanted them so badly, but when I accomplished them, they were not as satisfying.

During Christmas 2014 my eldest son had gone to spend time with his paternal grandmother out of town. This was a welcome break for me, but several days turned into a week and then into two weeks, and I missed him. So I called him:

Me: Ki, I miss you! When are you coming home?

Ki: I don't want to come home.

Me: What are you talking about? You need to come home, it's been too long.

Ki: I don't want to live with you anymore Mama, you are always stressed, always in front of the computer. You're not nice!

My sister had lost her son, and that day I realized that I had almost lost my son as well. After pleading and begging, my son finally agreed to come home. But I was crushed. What had I been doing? I vowed to be a better person, and that very night, I performed salat for the first time in a very long time. I sat on the floor in the dark and cried. I begged God for guidance and help. I remember the sense of comfort and warmth I felt as I put my head down on the floor and sobbed. It had been too long since I had prayed to God.

I had never been religious. My knowledge of Islam was also very rusty, so I started literally from zero. I decided I was going to be a Muslim with no affiliation and find the teachings that would make the most sense to me. My Quran had been relegated to a dusty corner on top of my bookcase. I dusted it and started reading every day. I gave away what were once my cherished brand-name possessions. I fasted and decided to sponsor a child. And I decided to wear the hijab. My husband was concerned, obviously because of the negativity that would ensue. But I was determined to follow the Quranic injunction to be modest.

I felt better about my body. I had struggled with an eating disorder in the past and the hijab liberated me from vanity. But I was subjected to a barrage of verbal abuse and comments from friends and colleagues. One female colleague told me, "You are embarrassing me, take that off." A friend said, "You don't look like a Muslim." It takes a strong heart and a thick skin to wear a hijab. So far I have been yelled at in the bus, called ISIS, called garbage, jeered at in a supermarket, and told to stop having kids (in front of my children, of course).

I wanted to learn more about Islam, so I explored YouTube channels and found hundreds of interesting sermons by clerics, on the subject of how to be a better Muslim. I chose two famous clerics to learn from. I thought to myself, "This is it, I have my Islam figured out." Was I wrong!

As I learned more, I stumbled into the issue of apostasy, which means recanting or the abandoning of one's faith. There had been a large uproar in the media amidst claims that Islam promotes the punishment of death for apostates. I knew this could not be true, since I had read in the Quran that there is no value in a faith that is forced upon someone. There is even a verse about a person who turned apostate, returned to Islam, and then turned apostate again, doing this several times without any worldly sanction (4:138). When I watched a famous scholar I had followed on video supporting the death penalty for apostates, I was truly shocked. Had I not been reading the Quran and learning about Islam myself, I would not have known about the erroneous understanding of Islam that is promoted by many scholars. It is not surprising that a captured Boko Haram leader could not recite the Quran, and that Daesh recruits had to buy the book *Islam for Dummies*. This group has not only busied itself with razing ancient churches and monasteries, kidnapping women, and killing non-Muslims; they have waged war against Muslims of all sects who do not support their Caliphate. In their online magazine *Dabiq*, Daesh calls for the extermination of the entire Shia Muslim population. Daesh is indeed Islam's worst enemy.

One night in 2015 I had a powerful dream. In my dream a woman approached me and asked for money. I looked at my wallet and saw a five-dollar bill and a ten-dollar bill. I gave her the five-dollar bill and she left. However, I felt bad because I realized I could have given her the ten-dollar bill instead, so I ran after her and followed her as she entered a building.

Inside I saw a glittering room with golden walls and crystal chandeliers. There were beautiful women with extravagant clothes. There were men in suits talking on their cellphones, and everyone seemed busy and occupied. I felt disturbed by the extravagant materialism on display, so I looked down and closed my eyes. As I closed my eyes, everything turned dark, but then suddenly, two candles appeared, one in front of each of my eyes. I noticed that the right candle shone brighter and the flame sparked. The spark took my breath away and then I was transported to a room covered from ceiling to floor in glass. In this room, I was standing and performing prayers with my family. As I prayed, I felt a force pulling me to look up, and when I looked up I saw and was embraced by a most beautiful shining light.

My dream began to come true as I rejected excessive materialism and focussed on spirituality. I took the opportunity to help and donate my money as much as I could, and at every step my prayers were answered. Now I thank Allah every single day for blessing me and giving me another chance. I am proud to serve Canada as a scholar and a woman. I echo the prayers of the late Mirza Tahir Ahmad, the fourth Caliph of the Ahmadiyya Muslim community: "May Canada become the whole world, and the whole world become Canada."

> And He found thee wandering in search for Him and
> guided thee unto Himself (Quran 93:8)

Contributors

ASHI MUNIR was born and raised in Toronto, her parents having come to Canada in the mid 1970s. She found it a struggle trying to figure out where she stood between two cultures.

After almost a decade in financial services, she made a shift into health information management. She has always enjoyed writing and saw this anthology as an opportunity to bring her experiences to light.

AZMINA KASSAM was born in Nairobi, Kenya and has lived in Vancouver, BC for over thirty years. She has taken numerous writing workshops and programs that have helped her to develop her writing capabilities. She is presently enrolled in the Creative Writing Program at Simon Fraser University. She believes that writing allows one an intimate lens into the spaces that are intimate and private so that "we may realize our common humanity through these words and these stories."

CARMEN TAHA JARRAH is a writer, human rights activist and international volunteer. She was born in Brazil to Lebanese parents who immigrated to Canada when she was still a child. She holds a Bachelor of Applied Communications in

Professional Writing and a first degree black belt in Tae Kwon Do. She has travelled extensively throughout the Middle East, Africa, the Indian subcontinent and Southeast Asia. Carmen is the author of *Smuggled Stories from the Holy Land* (2015), based on her experiences as a peace activist and volunteer olive picker in Palestine. She is currently working on her next book, about growing up Muslim in a small Canadian town.

DUAA AL-AGHAR is from Baghdad Iraq. She has master's degree in computer engineering and works as a webmaster. She is married and has two lovely kids. Her dream is to continue her education and get a PhD.

FERRUKH FARUQUI grew up in Winnipeg at a time when Canadian Muslims were for the most part invisible and voiceless. Over the ensuing decades, she's been struck by the changing and not always welcoming spiritual landscape of this burgeoning community. At the same time, she's observed the once unassailable standards of Canadian institutions sometimes falter in the face of an unrelentingly challenging global geopolitical reality that often questions the very humanity of Islam and its adherents. In her story, she writes of the divine spirit that permeates this vast land and nurtures her own faith.

GHAZIA SIRTAJ has joined York University in Toronto to complete her undergraduate degree; she hopes to go to graduate school. She is also managing a tedious divorce and is able to see her kids frequently. Ghazia is a woman with a passion for living who refuses to give up.

HANAN ABDULMALIK's professional portfolio began in Ethiopia and has been enriched by people and organizations around the globe. As a coordinator, organizer, project manager, and researcher, she has led global training projects with the United Nations, the Canadian government, and organizations aiming to use learning and education to improve the conditions of people and places everywhere. Hanan currently works from Mississauga, Ontario, where she contributes to a community collective homeschool.

 JENNA M EVANS is a researcher at the Institute of Health Policy, Management and Evaluation at the University of Toronto, and a certified health executive with the Canadian College of Health Leaders. Her research focuses on improving collaboration among professionals and organizations in the healthcare system. Jenna is also an avid volunteer with the Girl Guides of Canada and enjoys scrapbooking, reading historical fiction, and spending time outdoors.

 KIRSTIN SABRINA DANE is the writer behind "wood turtle," an internationally recognized blog on Muslim feminism and motherhood. Her work has been featured on *Muslimah Media Watch*, *Ms Magazine Blog*, *BlogHer*, *Bitch Media*, and the *Huffington Post*. Kirstin lives in the suburbs of Toronto with her family, makes Steampunk jewelry, and often gets her hijab in a bunch when negotiating faith, feminism, and motherhood.

 LAILA RE was born in Kabul, Afghanistan. She escaped from her native land with her family and lived as a refugee in Islamabad, Pakistan until her family immigrated to Canada in 1991. Laila has lived in Toronto since the age of five. She has self-published two books of poetry, *Pieces to Peace* and *Soul Led*. She earned her BA, B Ed, and M Ed at York University.

 LINA KHATIB, born in Calgary, living in Toronto, is the daughter of Syrian refugees to Canada. She holds an MPA degree from Queen's University, and has developed policy recommendations for various institutions, government, academic, and not-for-profit, particularly in the areas of immigration, education, and poverty reduction. Lina loves to write and enjoys

teaching writing techniques to youth and Canadian newcomers in her volunteer work.

MARIA CRUZ. When she's not working, volunteering, or cussing at stuff she has trouble using, Maria Cruz is usually swimming, sleeping, listening to audiobooks (thrillers and horror novels are her favourites), or trying to find ways she can make a positive difference. She's also a fan of conscious hip-hop and other music with great beats and decent lyrics. She hopes to get a manual wheelchair soon so she can burn some rubber in charity walks and runs.

MARIAM HAMAOUI graduated with a Specialized Honours in Religious Studies from York University. She currently works at Osgoode Hall, York University as the project associate and student liaison of the Syria Response and Refugee Initiative. She is also a settlement counsellor at Polycultural Immigrant and Community Services, helping Syrian refugees resettle in Toronto. She is the President of RefugeAid, an organization designed to raise awareness for refugees and asylum seekers around the world.

MARYAM KHAN is a PhD candidate in social work at York University, Canada. Her research interests include: race and racialization, sex work, Islam and sexual diversity, intersectional identities and identity politics, gender and sexuality, anticolonial thought and decolonization.

MEHAROONA GHANI was born and raised in Golden, BC and holds an MA in Gender and Development from the Institute of Development Studies in the UK. Now living in Vancouver, she is the former director of multiculturalism and antiracism programs in the BC Provincial Government and is now Community Engagement and Diversity Specialist, Spoken Word Facilitator, Educator and Writer with M Ghani Consulting. A graduate of Simon Fraser University's Writer's Studio (2013) and the Vancouver Manuscript Intensive (2014), Meharoona has been featured in six anthologies and has won competitions with the Surrey International Writers' Conference and the Poetry Institute of Canada. She is working on her first book: "Letters to Rumi."

MONA HASHIM was born in Egypt and lived in the Netherlands before coming to Canada. She is a mother of two children and stayed home for eight years to raise them. She has worked in employment counselling and settlement with newcomers and refugees. As a young girl she played the keyboard, loved photography and drawing, and wrote poems and stories. With her children finally grown up, she has revisited her old hobbies and writes short stories. She is working towards publishing her own book.

MUNIRAH MACLEAN is from London, England, where she studied comparative religion, philosophy, and education. After university she travelled to Sri Lanka to become a Buddhist nun. She met her soul mate, Dr Ibrahim Kreps, on a mountain in the Swiss Alps, took Shahadah with Sheikh Nazim al-Qubrusi in 1984, and arrived in Canada in 1985. She is the mother of three daughters. She has continued her spiritual travels and studies, and now runs a daycare and conducts mindfulness workshops.

SADIA KHAN was born in Wah Cantt, Pakistan. She received her bachelors degree in biology and chemistry and a master's degree in chemistry from Pakistan, following which she got married and came to Canada in 1994. She works for the Toronto District and Durham District School Boards and is a mother of three.

TAMMARA SOMA was born in Indonesia. She is a Pierre Elliott Trudeau 2014 Scholar and a doctoral candidate in Urban Planning at the University of Toronto. Tammara's academic research involves urban household food consumption and food wasting practices in Indonesia. Blessed with three beautiful children and a soulful musician as her husband, she hopes to demystify the teachings of Islam in Canada and help remove misconceptions about Muslims. Tammara is passionate about social justice, sustainable food, and indigenous justice; she is a member of the Indigenous Desk of the Ahmadiyya Muslim Community.

YASMINE MALLICK dedicates her life to teaching and mental health advocacy.

ZUNERA ISHAQ was born in Pakistan and lives in Mississauga, Ontario. In 2015 she became known for challenging the Conservative Canadian government's policy on wearing niqab at the citizenship ceremony, a controversial issue during that year's October federal election, in which the government lost. Before the election she was able to take the oath wearing a niqab, which is now a part of the Museums of Mississauga. She was selected as one of the 50 most influential people of 2015 throughout Toronto by *Toronto Life*.

About the Editor

SAIMA S HUSSAIN earned an honours BA in English and history and an MA in South Asian Studies from the University of Toronto. She worked as an admissions counsellor at the University of Toronto, then moved to Pakistan where she became books editor at *Dawn* newspaper. Upon returning to Canada she produced a history book for young readers, *The Arab World Thought of It: Inventions, Innovations and Amazing Facts* (Annick Press, 2013), which received an award from the Carolina Center for the Study of the Middle East and Muslim Civilizations. Saima is actively involved in arts and community projects and volunteers as a board member of the Canadian Council of Muslim Women. Photo by AliphAurMeem Photos.